LOVE WINS

"Lalita!" he exclaimed. As he spoke, a flash of lightning revealed her frightened face framed by her fair hair. The next thing Lord Heywood knew, Lalita was clinging to him. He could feel her trembling. "It is all right," he said soothingly.

"I . . . I am afraid it will . . . hit the house," she said. Lightning once again lit up the room and the thunder vibrated through it almost simultaneously.

Instinctively Lord Heywood tightened his arms and drew her closer still, and as he did so he realised that he loved her. As she raised her face to ask a question, lightning made Lord Heywood see her frightened eyes, her face very pale and her lips parted.

Because he could not help himself, he turned towards her and his lips came down on hers.

I am his, she thought, I have always . . . been his.

Bantam Books by Barbara Cartland
Ask your bookseller for the books you have missed

Barbara Cartland's Library of Love Series
THE OBSTACLE RACE

About Barbara Cartland
CRUSADER IN PINK

Love
Wins

Barbara Cartland

BANTAM BOOKS
TORONTO · NEW YORK · LONDON · SYDNEY

LOVE WINS

A Bantam Book / January 1982

ISBN   0-553-20235-9

Published simultaneously in the United States and Canada

Bantam Books are published by Bantam Books, Inc. Its trademark,
consisting of the words "Bantam Books" and the portrayal of a rooster,
is Registered in U.S. Patent and Trademark Office and in other
countries. Marca Registrada. Bantam Books, Inc., 666 Fifth Avenue,
New York, New York 10103.

Author's Note

As I write this I see in the newspapers that four drawings by Constable, found wrapped in brown paper in an attic, fetched nineteen thousand pounds yesterday at Sotheby's.

The great houses of England were filled with treasures in the seventeenth and eighteenth centuries because their owners were ardent collectors. Anxious to preserve these collections for posterity, they entailed their possessions onto the future holder of the title *ad infinitum*.

So many of my friends, pleading poverty after the wars, searched their huge ancestral homes for something to sell. One couple discovered a priceless pair of Chinese jade vases in a servant's bedroom. Another found that boots were cleaned on a table which was a perfect example of Queen Anne oyster walnut.

In the 1920s, while showing me a Chinese cabinet my host accidentally touched a secret drawer which disclosed a pearl necklace. It was nearly green with age, but it recovered its lovely shine when worn next to the skin.

Christie's opened their Sales-Rooms in Pall Mall in 1766 to compete with Sotheby's, who had opened in 1744. There were at one time sixty auctioneers handling the pictures and furniture which noblemen wished to sell.

Yet even the best valuers sometimes make a mistake. The Earl of Caledon sold the contents of his house a few miles from mine. His daughter was staying with me and we attended the sale. I was not very interested in a small ivory crucifix which was knocked down at seventeen pounds. It was subsequently discovered to be unique and was bought by the Victoria and Albert Museum for a sum exceeding six figures!

Chapter One

1817

The quay at Dover was in chaos.

There were three ships unloading at the same time and others waiting for a place.

It seemed impossible for anybody to put down another pin on the soil of England.

There was a melee of guns, boxes of ammunition, trunks, bales, harness and saddles, besides horses, dizzy and still trembling from the terror of the sea, while the grooms attending to them seemed in much the same condition.

Stretchers were being carried ashore with men who were wounded and seemed on the point of dying, and others, legless or armless, were being assisted by Orderlies who did not seem in much better shape themselves.

Besides which there were troopers who had lost their weapons and their kit-bags, and Sergeant-Majors roaring orders to which nobody appeared to listen.

"If this is peace," Colonel Romney Wood thought as

he stepped down the rickety gang-plank, "at least war was better organised."

At the same time, although he told himself he was being sentimental, he could not help a thrill of excitement that he was home after six long years of war in enemy territory.

Like most of the British Army he had hoped that after Waterloo and Napoleon's exile to St. Helena they would be able to return home, but the Army of Occupation was, in the Duke of Wellington's opinion, essential to the peace of Europe.

At first Colonel Wood had thought his Commander-in-Chief's insistence on it was unsubstantiated, especially after the capitulation of Paris without further fighting.

But Wellington had no thought of interfering with the future French Civil Government. He was occupied, as always after a battle, with protecting civilians from Military excesses.

The Prussians, however, saw nothing wrong in reprisals, and the difference between the British and their allies had become evident as soon as the Battle of Waterloo had been won.

Romney Wood had done his best not to become involved in political issues, but the Duke of Wellington was fond of him and knew he was an exceptional man and undoubtedly one of his best Officers.

He therefore found himself not only looking after his own troops but being constantly sent off by Wellington to cope with the difficulties which appeared all too frequently like spectres to spoil the triumph of victory.

"Dammit all!" Colonel Wood's younger Officers said to him almost daily. "What did we fight for, if it was not to defeat Napoleon and be allowed to go home?"

They could not find any reason for the Duke's insistence on an Army of Occupation, and they agreed with the French that the feeding of 150,000 men would require a miracle of organisation.

The Duke had sent for Romney Wood.

"They want me to send home thirty thousand men forthwith," he said abruptly.

"I heard, Your Grace, that was the number that had been decided upon."

"Decided!" the Duke said testily. "I am the one to do the deciding!"

"Of course," Romney Wood agreed.

"I have already brought the Army down to one hundred fifty thousand by sending home eight hundred men," the Duke grumbled.

Romney Wood said nothing.

He knew that the politicians in both countries were not going to think that enough. In January 1817 the Duke had said to the permanent conference of four Ambassadors:

"I confess that my opinion has altered and I would propose a reduction of thirty thousand men to begin on the first of April."

It was, most people agreed, a step in the right direction, but *Madame* de Staël and a large number of very attractive women were using every variety of allure in their repertoire to bring about the total end of the Occupation.

However, hopes were dashed when, as usual, dilatory Cabinets kept changing their minds.

The Duke of Wellington had showed Colonel Wood a letter from the Earl of Bathurst which said:

Popular impatience in France to get rid of foreigners does not inspire me with a corresponding wish to leave.

Romney Wood had laughed.

"I know exactly what you are feeling, Your Grace. At the same time, it would be a mistake to out-stay our welcome to the point where it becomes a 'retreat.' "

The Duke nodded.

He knew, as Romney Wood did, that the hostility between the French and British Officers was an increasing problem.

But now at last, after more and more difficulties, a large number of the British Army were back on their native soil.

Romney Wood thought as he crossed the Channel that the last three years had not been particularly pleasant ones.

There had undoubtedly been moments of enjoyment, especially in Paris, where from a social point of view things had got back to normal far quicker than might have been expected.

However, as he told himself over and over again, he had no wish for poodle-faking and preferred the battlefield to the *Boudoir* and the roar of guns to the waltz.

At the same time, after enduring privations and desperate fighting both in Portugal and in France, he had found both the food of Paris and its beautiful women something he could not ignore, even though there was something cynical in his regard of them.

What really perturbed him was that he would from today cease to be a soldier.

He had sent in his papers and said farewell to the Duke before he had left France.

"I shall miss you," Wellington had said briefly, but with a sincerity that was undeniable.

"My father died two years ago," he replied to the Duke, "and it is therefore essential that I should go home and see to my own affairs."

"Good Heavens!" the Commander-in-Chief exclaimed. "I had forgotten you are now Lord Heywood!"

"I had no wish to use my title while I was still soldiering," Colonel Wood replied, "but I know Your Grace will understand that as I was an only child there is nobody to see to the Estate in my absence, and in fact I have not set foot in England for six years."

The Duke had not demurred after that, but Romney Wood had known with an ache in his heart how much he would miss the men with whom he had served for so long and the friendships he had made in war, which in peace would never be the same.

"I am home!" he tried to console himself as he picked his way among the debris on the quay.

Then his sentimental feelings were forgotten as he cursed a porter for running into him with a truck.

There was no possibility of getting away from Dover that night, and it was only the fact of his superior rank, combined with his air of authority and his exceptional good looks, which enabled him to find a room in which to sleep.

The following morning there were innumerable problems brought to him by men of his own Regiment which he was obliged to help them to solve before he left.

He had also to conduct a personal interview, but with the general confusion in the Hotel as well as in the streets, it was difficult to find a place where he could have a quiet conversation.

Having made up his mind before he left France that he would not go to London, but having arrived in England would ride home across country, he had written to his family Solicitors to send a representative to meet him at Dover.

He had no idea how difficult it would be not only to

find the man who was waiting for him with a somewhat glazed expression on his face in the foyer of a Hotel which was packed to suffocation with Officers, but to find a room where they could talk without having to shout above the noise of a hundred other voices.

Finally the Manager offered Romney Wood the use of his own private Office, and when he shut the door it seemed for the moment to be an oasis of quiet.

"I had no idea when I asked you to come down from London, Mr. Crosswaith," Lord Heywood told the Solicitor, "that the conditions at Dover would be so chaotic."

"That is understandable, My Lord, in the circumstances," Mr. Crosswaith replied.

He was a small, dried-up-looking man nearing old age, with white hair and wearing glasses, and Romney Wood thought with a faint smile that he would have recognised him as being a Solicitor anywhere and in any company.

"First," Lord Heywood said as Mr. Crosswaith sat down, clutching his bulging brief-case, "I should thank you for the letters you wrote me when I was in France. I found, however, that those I received in the last eighteen months were somewhat depressing."

"That is not surprising, My Lord," Mr. Crosswaith replied. "Many young men like yourself when they have left the Army are being unpleasantly surprised with the conditions in England."

"I had heard that the war-time economy had collapsed in poverty and suffering," Lord Heywood said sharply.

"It is true," Mr. Crosswaith agreed, "and I will not disguise the fact from Your Lordship that there is a great deal of distress and social unrest throughout the country."

This was something Lord Heywood had already learnt from the Duke, who had paid a flying visit to England.

"Things are rough," he had said sharply. "Starving agricultural labourers are being hanged, but food-shops being gutted and machines being wrecked by Luddites do not solve anything."

However, Lord Heywood was at the moment concerned with his own personal problem.

"What I gathered from your last letter, Mr. Crosswaith," he said, "is that the Heywood Estate is almost bankrupt."

"It is not a word I like to use, My Lord," the Solicitor replied, "but it is an unfortunate fact that the farmers cannot pay their rent because they are making no money, and unless Your Lordship has some source of income which has not been revealed to me, it will be hard to decide what you can do in the immediate future."

"As bad as that?" Lord Heywood enquired.

He knew what the answer would be before Mr. Crosswaith replied:

"Worse!"

"Very well," he said. "We now have to decide what we can sell."

"I anticipated that was a question Your Lordship would ask," Mr. Crosswaith replied in his prim voice. "I have therefore made a list of the assets available. I am afraid there are very few."

Lord Heywood frowned.

"What do you mean—few?"

Mr. Crosswaith coughed apologetically.

"Your Lordship must be aware that your grandfather, the fifth Baron, tied up everything that the family possessed in an entail which is impossible to break without there being three direct heirs to the Estate alive at the same time."

7

"I had no idea of that."

"I have brought the deeds for Your Lordship to see."

"I am quite prepared to take your word for it, Mr. Crosswaith. What you are saying is that I cannot sell Heywood House in London or Heywood Abbey in the country, and little or none of their contents."

"That is the exact position, My Lord," Mr. Crosswaith said.

He spoke in a tone of satisfaction because he had not had to spell out the bad news in detail himself.

Lord Heywood drummed his fingers on the deal-table which the Manager of the Hotel used as a desk.

It was stained with alcohol which had been upset and with ink, and scarred with the rough edges of pewter pots, but Lord Heywood did not notice.

He was actually wondering how he was going to live on nothing, for that was what the news that Crosswaith had brought him amounted to.

Looking back, he could remember how flourishing the Heywood Estate in Buckinghamshire where he had been brought up had seemed when he was a boy.

The farmers had been prosperous, the labourers smiling and happy. At the Abbey the stables had been filled with horses and there had been half-a-dozen tall young footmen in attendance in the pillared Hall.

Outside, a whole army of gardeners, stable-hands, stone-masons, carpenters, woodmen, keepers, and foresters made the Heywood Estate one of the most enviable possessions in the country.

It did not seem possible that everything should have collapsed like a gas-filled balloon and there was nothing left.

He told himself it was impossible and he would find that Mr. Crosswaith was exaggerating.

"I promise you I have been into it very carefully, My

Lord, in both the main houses, besides counting the other assets on the Estate itself. But once again I am afraid there is little or nothing Your Lordship can sell."

"What about trees?"

"Those that were of any use were cut down during the early years of the war. Those that remain are either too old or too young and are not suitable for ships' timbers or for building houses."

"There must be something!" Lord Heywood said, and however much he tried to control it there was a note of desperation in his voice.

He was aware that he himself was in debt. It was for quite a large sum because there had been considerable drains on his purse this past year.

It was not, as people might have supposed, because he had spent money on the beautiful but greedy women with whom Paris abounded, but because he had helped so many of his brother-officers whom he had considered at the time to be in a far worse plight then he was himself.

"I shall arrive home without a penny to bless myself with!" one of his men had complained bitterly.

"Bust, broke, below hatches," another and younger man had told him. "This is what comes of fighting for your King and country, while those who remained at home are living off the fat of the land."

There had been a loan here and a loan there that he had never expected to see again, but it was a price that Lord Heywood had paid gladly for the friendship, the obedience, and the admiration the younger men had given him both in war and during the years of Occupation.

Now he knew that he had been too generous and had forgotten his obligations to his own people, the people whose whole lives centered round the big house.

He was aware that Mr. Crosswaith was looking at him with worried eyes.

"I shall wait until I get home to the Abbey," he said, "and see what can be done. But are you telling me there is nothing in the Bank?"

"My Partner and I, My Lord, carried out your wishes after your father's death by paying the pensioners and the wages of those servants who stayed on until they could find other employment."

"How many are left in London?" Lord Heywood asked.

"There are the Butler and his wife, who are really too old and should be pensioned if there was a cottage available for them, and the boot-boy who is seventy-three, and the odd-job man who I should imagine is getting on for eighty."

"And in the country?"

"Fortunately, almost all of the servants have found other jobs," Mr. Crosswaith replied. "The only two left are Merrivale and his wife; you may remember he was a footman in your grandfather's time and later became Butler to your father."

"Yes, I know Merrivale," Lord Heywood said.

"He is a very old man now and he and his wife were appointed caretakers of the Abbey. They live in a cottage in the stable-yard."

"Is that all?"

"Grimshaw the Head Groom died last year and so did Evans the gardener. Their wives are both deceased."

"So there are only the Merrivales left at the Abbey?"

"That is so, My Lord, but you will appreciate there was no money with which to pay new servants, and anyway it seemed to us to be an extravagance until we knew when Your Lordship was returning."

"You are quite right," Lord Heywood said. "And now, for what can be sold."

He put out his hand as he spoke and Mr. Crosswaith put a sheet of paper into it.

On it were written a dozen items in a clear hand.

"This is all?"

"I am afraid so, My Lord. The furniture in the State bedrooms, together with the paintings and the silver, are of course entailed, and anything else in the house, such as curtains, carpets, and furniture in the minor rooms, would not be saleable at this moment except for such a small sum that it would hardly be worth mentioning."

"And the same applies in London?"

"Exactly the same, My Lord."

Lord Heywood's lips tightened. Then he said:

"I need not ask if there are any purchasers for land these days, and farms in particular."

"There's a glut on the market," Mr. Crosswaith answered. "Every Landlord is trying to dispose of his farms because they are unproductive. The Corn Laws which were passed to keep out cheap foreign corn have only resulted in more starvation without there being any prospect of the farmers getting an economic price for what they produce."

Lord Heywood wanted to remark that this was the spoils of victory, but he thought it would seem a cheap expression which he had heard so often from other people and so he said nothing.

Then as Mr. Crosswaith closed his brief-case he said:

"I only wish, My Lord, that I'd been able to bring you happier tidings. If it is your wish, my Partners and I'll have another look at the house in London, but the only person who appears to be buying anything these days is His Royal Highness the Prince Regent, and as he never pays his debts, most gentlemen are not anxious to sell him their possessions."

Lord Heywood rose to his feet.

"What I intend to do, Mr. Crosswaith," he said, "is to ride from here to the Abbey. When I have inspected the conditions I find there and come to some conclusion as to what can be done in the future, I will of course communicate with you."

"Thank you, My Lord."

"I am extremely grateful for the way in which you have administered the Estates in my absence, and I know I can trust you to carry on in the future."

"We are deeply grateful for Your Lordship's patronage."

Lord Heywood did not mention that it was doubtful if the firm would ever be paid their fees, but he realised that one person who was well aware of that was Mr. Crosswaith himself.

The Solicitor bowed himself from the Office and Lord Heywood sat for some minutes with unseeing eyes.

He wondered in fact what the devil he was going to do, then he told himself in a practical manner that there was no use in planning anything until he had seen the condition of the Abbey and the Estate.

He realised as he looked down at the table that Mr. Crosswaith had left behind a large stack of papers and that the most bulky of them was the Inventory of Heywood Abbey, and another was entitled: *The Contents of Heywood House*.

"There must be something!" he murmured.

At the same time, he did not feel very optimistic, but it was in fact some consolation to realise that he had about twenty pounds in cash on him.

It had come from the sale at a ridiculously small price to an avaricious French Dealer of the possessions he had accumulated in Paris during the time he had been there at Wellington's beck and call.

Lord Heywood thought he would have preferred to be camping in a tent with his men or in the Barracks they had commandeered on the outskirts of the City.

He had actually divided his time between several different places.

Now he thought that for all he had been able to do he should have returned home earlier. In fact, if he had sold out at the moment the news of his father's death had reached him, he might have been in a better position now to salvage some of the farms on the Estate.

But it was too late for regrets. All he could do was to go home and see the difficulties for himself.

*   *   *

It was very early the next morning when Lord Heywood and his Batman, Carter, rode onto the Heywood Estate.

It had been so difficult to get away from Dover that, although they had travelled as fast as their horses could carry them, they had finally been overtaken by darkness and been forced to put up at a wayside Inn.

It had been rough and uncomfortable and Lord Heywood's charger had seemed out-of-place in the small broken-down stables in which there was hardly room for the horse which Carter rode.

They persuaded the Innkeeper to find them some fresh straw, and as dawn broke Lord Heywood thought the horses would doubtless have been more comfortable than he had been.

However, he had not complained because bivouacking on a barren mountain in Portugal had taught him that there were varying degrees of comfort.

However, he had no wish to linger on a mattress that

seemed to be composed of hard rocks, and he had risen at first light to find that Carter was already up and grooming the horses.

Breakfast consisted of some stale bread, a lump of hard cheese, and some butter which smelt rancid.

"I will wait until I get home," Lord Heywood remarked, pushing it aside, and having paid the Inn-keeper they were on their way.

As he rode on the land that was familiar to him Lord Heywood remembered once again the thrill that he had tried to deny when he had set foot on British soil at Dover.

Now the soil was his, part of his blood, his heritage, and part too of his childhood and of so many memories that he thought he had forgotten.

He found himself remembering isolated incidents almost as if they were pictures in front of his eyes.

He could see the first fish he had ever caught in the lake fighting at the end of his line, and he could feel the cold of the water as he swam, though he was forbidden to do so, amongst the swans who swept away disdainfully because he was disturbing their serenity.

He remembered the first pigeon he had shot and how he had carried it home in pride to show his father.

After that there had been his first rabbit, his first partridge, his first pheasant, and, more exciting than anything else, his first pony when he was almost too small to walk, and later a larger pony and then horses, always horses that he thought carried him swifter than the wind.

These memories, like the land on which he was riding, were in his breathing and living and he knew that whatever happened in the future it was his, and he could not lose it nor would he leave it.

He had said to Carter the previous day:

"If you come with me, life is going to be uncomfortable. England is not the same as when we left it, and for all I know at the moment I may not even be able to afford to eat, let alone feed you."

He paused before he added:

"Quite frankly, I have not the faintest idea where your wages are to come from!"

"Don't you worry about that, Sir," Carter replied. "We managed some'ow when we was a-fightin', an' as for food, I dare say as 'ow I can forage some."

Lord Heywood laughed.

"If you do, you will find yourself being hanged or transported for stealing anything over a shilling in value. It is not an enemy we have to cope with now, but the English Law!"

Carter had grinned in a manner which was an impudence in itself.

"I al'ays thought 'twere a blessin' them Frenchy farmers was such bad shots!"

Lord Heywood did not reply because he thought it undignified to do so.

If he had told Carter once, he had told him a dozen times that the English, unlike the French, always paid for anything they took from the inhabitants of the country over which they were fighting.

On many occasions he had gone back to a farm from which Carter had purloined a couple of hens or a young lamb to pay an infuriated and extremely hostile farmer.

But they had on the whole been so surprised at the honesty of the British that they had accepted the money with alacrity and at the same time were suspicious of an ulterior motive behind the offer.

"You will, I hope, find plenty of rabbits and game on the Estate," Lord Heywood said aloud, "which are mine, and yours if you can catch or shoot them, provided we are able to afford cartridges."

However, as they rode he thought he did not see as many rabbits and hares as he expected, nor was there any sign of the pheasants which had once bred profusely in the woods.

He suspected that since there were no game-keepers to keep a watch there had been plenty of locals who were prepared to risk the heavy penalties of being caught rather than remain hungry.

"Surely things cannot be so bad in the country?" Lord Heywood asked himself, and he knew this was another question to which he must find an answer.

It was still very early and the mist was hanging over the lake when finally they came in sight of the house.

Heywood Abbey had been built originally by Cistercian Monks, but practically nothing of the original Abbey remained.

It was the second Lord Heywood who had commissioned Robert Adam when he was still a young man to build him a house which he considered was the right background for his considerable pretensions.

It was therefore an extremely impressive building, with a centre block rising to a roof decorated with urns and statues and with two wings stretching out on either side.

It had an exquisite, artistic symmetry which in the years to come was to make Robert Adam the most famous architect of the period.

Now in the pale sunshine it looked so lovely and at the same time so magnificent that it was impossible for Lord Heywood to realise not only that it was empty but he could not afford to pay even one servant to attend to his needs.

Almost instinctively he had drawn in his horse and Carter had done the same.

There was a silence. Then Carter said:

"Be that yours, Sir?"

"That is my home, Carter."

Carter scratched the side of his head.

"Looks like a Barracks ter me!"

Lord Heywood laughed.

He was aware that Carter was a Cockney by birth, and when he had joined the Army, ostensibly because he had a sense of adventure, he would never have imagined that one man would require such a large building to house him.

Then Lord Heywood knew that if this was where he intended to live, he needed Carter more than he had ever needed anybody before.

It was not only his ability to make the best of any situation in which they found themselves, and his gift of procuring food like manna from Heaven from the most unlikely places, which made him such an asset.

It was his cheerfulness and his sense of humour, and Lord Heywood would have been very stupid if he had not realised that Carter in his own way almost worshipped him.

An orphan brought up in a Charity School and apprenticed to a man who had ill-treated him and from whom he had run away and then pitch-forked into the war, he looked upon Lord Heywood since they had been together in the Army as a Providence round whom his whole existence was centred.

"Barracks or not," he said aloud, "this is where you and I are going to live for the moment, and I promise you we shall be more comfortable than we were last night."

"Well, Sir, I s'pose we can make the best of it!"

Carter said cheerfully. "But we'll doubtless wear out our boots walkin' from one end of it t'other! And there won't be no Ordnance to go to for replacements!"

Lord Heywood laughed, then he touched his horse to make him move quicker towards his old home.

It was very quiet in the stables, and in the cottage where he knew Merrivale and his wife lived the curtains were still drawn over the windows.

Having put the horses in stalls that needed sweeping out and having unharnessed them and provided them with water, Lord Heywood and Carter walked towards the back-door of the house.

"We may not be able to get in," Lord Heywood said, "in which case we shall have to wake Merrivale. He is a very old man and I would rather wait to approach him when he is dressed, as it may give him a shock to see me."

"I'll find a way in, Sir—I mean, M'Lord."

He kept forgetting that his Master should be addressed by his new title.

However, Lord Heywood certainly made no difficulty about it.

The back-door was locked, but a window was half-open and Carter climbed in through it to find a larger and easier window through which his Master could follow him.

Lord Heywood felt it was a somewhat undignified way to enter his own home.

At the same time, he rather wanted to be alone for the first exlporation of it and not have to listen to long-winded chatter about what had and had not been done.

Having left Carter inspecting the kitchens to see if there was anything for breakfast, he walked away along the passage which was shut off by a baize door from the best part of the house.

All the curtains were drawn. There was a faint light percolating at the sides of them from a sun which had not yet fully risen.

In the dimness Lord Heywood felt that he was walking back in time and now he was a little boy thinking how large the rooms were and listening to the deepness of his father's voice and the soft tones of his mother's.

He looked into the huge Dining-Room, in the centre of which was a long table where it was easy to seat fifty people at once.

There was a thick layer of dust on everything, and because the thought that he would never be able to entertain here was depressing, he walked on.

He avoided the larger rooms and came to the small Drawing-Room which his father and mother had used every day, while the State-Rooms were kept for special occasions.

Here the curtains were closed and he could make out only the outlines of the furniture covered in Holland dust-sheets.

He walked on again and now he reached the door of the Library with its enormous array of books and the balcony up to which as a child he would climb a twisting ladder.

But instead of entering it he turned back to walk up the gilded and carved staircase to the First Floor.

In front of him was the Grand Salon, where he remembered his father and mother had entertained the Prince of Wales and had given parties to which the whole County had flocked as if in obedience to an Imperial Command.

Here also everything was shrouded in dust-sheets, and he told himself that later he would come back and open the heavy curtains and let in the sunlight.

It was almost like being at a Funeral to see everything shrouded and dark, and he walked on down the wide corridor seeking the Suite of rooms which had always been occupied by his parents.

He felt that by going to the bedroom where his father had died and where the head of the family had slept for generations he was paying his last respects to the parent he had loved.

He had not been aware of his father's death until two months after it had happened.

He had been fighting his way across France towards Belgium when the letter which had followed him for countless miles had finally reached his hand.

He had thought as he took it from the messenger that it was a despatch, then when he realised that it was in fact a letter from England he had at first placed it into a pocket of his tunic to read later.

Because it was very late before he went to bed that night, it was by the flickering light of the candle lantern in his tent that he had learnt his father was dead and he was now the fifth Lord Heywood.

The title had seemed of no importance at the time and he had deliberately continued to be known to his men, to his superiors, and even to the Duke of Wellington as Colonel Wood.

Lord Heywood opened the door of his father's bedroom, which seemed to him now as large as he remembered it, and walked to one of the windows to pull back the curtains.

The huge four-poster bed was still hung with crimson brocade and at its head the family coat-of-arms had been embroidered more than a century earlier by the wife of the second Baron after he had left her to go to the wars with Marlborough.

Lord Heywood remembered all the furniture and the paintings. Too, he recalled as a little boy thinking:

'One day I shall sleep here, and it will be like being in a big ship with crimson sails.'

He looked round him, feeling as if the spirit of his father was welcoming him home.

Then he went towards the communicating door which led into the room which had always been his mother's.

She too had died while he was serving in Portugal and there had been no chance of his returning home.

He thought now how lovely she had been and how even now he still missed her.

It was a pain he had not expected to find, that the house brought her back so vividly that he longed for her in a way that had something child-like about it.

He remembered somebody saying to him once:

"You are never grown up until your parents are both dead and you are on your own. Then you know you have become a man."

The communicating door would not open and Lord Heywood thought perhaps his father had locked it after his mother's death.

He walked back into the passage and tried the outer door but that too was locked.

He felt somehow annoyed that he was debarred from entering his mother's room as he wished to do, and he supposed he would have to ask Merrivale for the key.

Then he remembered that there was another way into the bedroom through his mother's *Boudoir*.

He walked a little farther down the passageway until he came to the door of the *Boudoir* and when he turned the handle it opened.

The curtains were drawn but the room unexpectedly felt fresh and fragrant.

However, without pausing to investigate the reason, he opened the communicating door and moved immediately towards one of the long windows hung with silk brocade curtains in a soft blue which had been one of his mother's favourite colours.

He pulled back one of the heavy curtains and saw to his surprise that the window was open and he felt the soft warm air on his face.

There was sunshine too, for while he had been inside the house the sun had risen and was now casting a golden glow over the gardens and dispersing the mist over the lake.

As Lord Heywood pulled back the other curtain, the sunlight flooded into the room and he turned to look at the large and beautiful bed that he remembered well with its gilded posts carved with flowers, and silk curtains draped from a canopy ornamented with doves and small fat cupids circling round a crown.

Even as he looked at the bed, feeling that it was part of the happiness of his childhood, something stirred.

For a moment he could hardly believe his eyes. Then as the bed-covering moved he was aware that there was a head against the pillow, and the next minute that moved too and somebody sat up.

There was a small, oval-shaped face with the faintly pink cheeks of a child who has been asleep.

There was long fair hair falling in disarray over a white diaphanous nightgown.

Then two large, very deep blue eyes were staring at Lord Heywood and a voice asked:

"Who are . . . you? What are you doing . . . here?"

Chapter Two

There was silence, as Lord Heywood was too astounded to reply.

Then he said:

"As your host, I should be asking you those questions."

The blue eyes opened if possible wider than ever.

"My . . . host? You . . . cannot be . . . Lord Heywood! He is . . . abroad."

"I have returned," Lord Heywood replied, "at what appears to be an inconvenient moment."

His visitor considered this for a moment, then she said:

"It will certainly be . . . inconvenient if you are . . . ordering me to . . . leave, which is something I . . . can not do . . . immediately."

"That is obvious," Lord Heywood remarked drily.

As he spoke he glanced at her nightgown, which was fine enough to be very revealing.

He could see the curves of two very young breasts, and as if she was suddenly aware of it she quickly pulled the sheet higher.

Lord Heywood noticed as she did so that the sheet edged with lace bore his mother's monogram, and the pillow-cases, also with a frill of real lace, were something he remembered.

"You have certainly made yourself very comfortable!" he remarked sarcastically.

"There was . . . nobody to . . . stop me, and the caretakers, if that is what those two old people are, never come . . . higher than the . . . ground floor."

Lord Heywood moved a little way from the window towards the bed, but not near enough to frighten this strange young woman.

Now that he could see her more clearly he realised she was very lovely, in fact far too beautiful to be wandering about apparently alone and sleeping in a strange house without anybody else's knowledge of it.

"Suppose we start at the beginning," he said. "As you know who I am, please tell me your name and why you are here."

There was a distinct pause and he knew from the expression on the girl's face that she was thinking.

He waited until she said a little hesitatingly:

"My . . . name is . . . Lalita!"

Lord Heywood again waited, and as she said no more he asked:

"And your other name?"

"As far as you need be . . . concerned, my name is Lalita . . . and that is . . . all."

"I suspect you have run away and are hiding."

She gave him a flashing smile.

"That is intelligent of you."

"Thank you," he said. "But the information you have given me is too scanty."

"That is all I can tell you."

"Why?"

"Because, as you so rightly surmised . . . I have run away, and as there was nobody living in this lovely house it seemed a . . . perfect place in which to . . . hide."

"From whom?"

Again she smiled and there was a hint of mischief in her blue eyes.

"That, as you must be aware, is a question I must not answer."

"Very well," Lord Heywood said. "As you are determined to be mysterious, will you tell me why you are hiding?"

Lalita put her head a little on one side and he realised with amusement that she was considering whether or not she could trust him.

After a moment he said:

"Shall I promise you that nothing you say at the moment will be used in evidence against you?"

Now she gave a little laugh and he thought it was an unexpectedly joyous sound.

"You are not a bit like I expected you to be," she said. "I looked at the paintings of all those pompous old ancestors of yours on the stairs and in the Dining-Room, and I thought you would be like them."

"I always believed there was a distinct family resemblance."

"It is very slight and you are much more handsome than I expected, and younger."

"I would accept that as a compliment if I did not think it was simply a means to an end."

Again she laughed.

"Of course it is! I want you to help me by letting me stay here."

"You must realise that is impossible."

Because he wished to see her better than he could at

the moment, Lord Heywood turned to draw back the curtains from one of the other windows.

Now the sunshine seemed to fill the room with a golden haze and he thought as he looked back to the bed that against the white linen and lace and the blue curtains Lalita was like a Princess in a fairy-tale.

She looked somehow insubstantial with her fair hair and blue eyes, and what he could see now was a flawless pink-and-white skin that made him feel that she was a figment of his imagination and had stepped out of a dream.

He deliberately sat down in one of the chairs with a gilt frame that was covered in blue brocade.

Then as he crossed his legs and appeared to be very much at his ease he said:

"If you want my help, then at least make your plea for it sound convincing."

She gave him a little glance from under her eyelashes, which he realised curled back from her blue eyes like a child's and were gold at the roots and became naturally dark at the tips.

"I suppose that is the way," she said, "you behave to your poor soldiers when they are up in front of you for being late on parade or some other dastardly crime."

"They usually have a very plausible excuse."

"Very well, I will tell you mine. I have run away because my Guardian is trying to marry me to an . . . imbecile."

Lord Heywood looked at her incredulously.

"It is true!" she said defensively.

"And why should your Guardian wish to do that?"

"Because the imbecile is his son!"

"I find that assertion hard to believe."

"So, I suspect, would everybody else," Lalita replied. "But I refuse, utterly and absolutely refuse, to marry a

26

man who is what the servants call 'touched in the attic' and who slobbers at me and has wet, flabby hands."

The way she spoke sounded so like a small animal spitting at its pursuers that Lord Heywood could not help laughing.

"It may seem funny to you," Lalita said, "but it was a case of either doing what my uncle wanted or running away."

"So it is your uncle who is your Guardian!" Lord Heywood said quietly.

"Now you are being sneaky and trying to get things out of me," Lalita retorted, "but I can promise you one thing: if you try to make me go back I shall either escape or drown myself in the lake."

"Very dramatic!" Lord Heywood exclaimed. "But you sound somewhat hysterical and that weakens your case."

Lalita gave a sound that was one of exasperation.

"Why did you have to come back?" she complained. "I found this a perfect place in which to hide and it was in fact . . . very comfortable."

"How did you feed yourself?"

She looked at him in a way that made him know she was deciding whether or not to tell him the truth.

Then she said:

"It has been somewhat of a monotonous diet. The caretakers keep hens who lay . . . all over the place, and there are plenty of . . . vegetables in the garden."

Lord Heywood's lips twitched.

"I see you are very resourceful."

"Actually I am a good cook when I have the ingredients, but when I ran away I had no idea where I was going and so I did not think of taking food with me."

"You must have had some idea where you were heading."

"I did think of going to France. Perhaps you could help me to do that."

"I do not think France is at all the right place for you at this moment," Lord Heywood said firmly.

"Why not? The war is over, and I am not only very proficient in French, but Mama had a close friend there called the *Duchesse* de Soissons, who I am sure would be glad to see me, if I could find her."

"Are you really contemplating wandering about France alone, looking for a *Duchesse* who may be dead for all you know?"

"I think it would be rather exciting!"

"You do not know what you are talking about."

As he spoke, Lord Heywood thought of the chaos in the country he had just left.

There were still deserters from the French Army pillaging and looting when they got the chance, and the peasants were desperately poor after the privations they had endured during the fighting.

There was also, as usual, an enormous amount of corruption.

He could not imagine anything nearer to madness than that a young woman alone and as pretty as Lalita should travel anywhere in France.

There was a thoughtful expression on his face and after a moment she said:

"Well, if you will not let me go to France . . . the alternative is to . . . stay here."

"That, as I have already said, is impossible!" Lord Heywood replied.

"But why? The house is big enough, and if you feel your friends might notice me, I could hide away in some small attic."

"I certainly do not mean to entertain," Lord Heywood said.

"Why not? There must be a lot of people willing to welcome you after being away for so long, now that you have returned home."

"A home I cannot afford!"

He had not meant to say anything so intimate but the words had come bitterly to his lips before he could prevent them.

"Are you saying that you are in the same position as all the other men who have come back from the war?" Lalita asked.

"It depends what you mean," Lord Heywood said cautiously, wishing he had not been so outspoken.

"But you must be aware," she replied, "that most of the men recently demobilised from the forces are desperately poor, many of them in rags, and they returned to find their homes with leaking roofs, their children hungry, and, needless to say, there is no work for them."

Lord Heywood was surprised not only that she knew what was happening but that there should be so much compassion in her voice, as if their suffering hurt her.

All the British women he had met in Paris since the war ended had been concerned only with the round of social activities designed to entertain them.

Though the Senior Officers talked of the unhappy conditions in England, it was not a subject of conversation at dinner-parties, and he had the feeling that if the poor were suffering, the rich did not care.

He realised that Lalita was waiting for an answer to her question, and after a moment he said:

"You have expressed my position very eloquently."

"But you have this house, although your farms are in a bad state like everybody else's."

"How do you know that?"

"I have seen them."

"When?"

"I am not going to answer that sort of question, as I realise you are trying to find out more about me."

"But you must understand that I cannot help you unless I have some idea of why you are here."

"I have told you that unless I go back and marry a man who makes me creep, there is nothing else I can do but throw myself on your mercy, since you will not let me go to France."

"Again very dramatically put," Lord Heywood said, "but impossible for a number of reasons. First because I can hardly be responsible for hiding a girl of your age without getting myself into a great deal of trouble, and secondly because I cannot afford to entertain a guest of any sort."

"I can pay my way. I have a little money with me."

"I have not yet reached the point where I have to accept money from a woman!" Lord Heywood said coldly.

"Hoity-toity!" Lalita mocked. "Beggars cannot be choosers!"

She thought perhaps she had annoyed him and added quickly:

"Not that I believe you really are a beggar when you own a house like this."

"It belongs, together with the Estates, to the future inheritor of the title," Lord Heywood said.

"You mean your son?"

"As things are, I think it is very unlikely that I shall ever be able to afford one."

"But you would like to be married?"

"Good God, no!" Lord Heywood ejaculated before he could stop himself. "I have enough troubles at the moment without that!"

"Splendid! Since that makes two of us who have no wish to get married, we should get along famously."

Lord Heywood sighed.

"Now listen, Lalita," he said, "before we embroil ourselves any further in this fantasy, we have to face facts. I am sorry for your difficulties, if they are what you say they are, but there is nothing I can do about them. I will see if my Batman can find us anything to eat, then you must be on your way."

"On my way to . . . where?"

"That is your business."

"How can you be so cold-hearted . . . so cruel . . . so brutal as to turn me . . . out when you know I have nowhere to go?"

"Perhaps you should go home, wherever that may be."

"And marry a man I loathe and detest? How could I let . . . him . . . touch me?"

Her voice had so much horror in it that almost despite himself Lord Heywood stiffened.

Now there was an expression on her face which he knew owed nothing to acting, and now he fully realised that she was frightened, really frightened of being forced into marriage with a man she obviously detested.

"I presume you are an orphan, but have you no other relatives who could help you?" he asked.

"I do not think they would be willing to hide me from my uncle."

"Who is your uncle?"

"I have no intention of telling you that, and if you were a gentleman you would not press me."

"If I had any common sense I would force you to tell me the truth. Then I would immediately inform your uncle so he could come and take you away."

"But instead will you . . . try to understand how desperate . . . I am?"

The question was undoubtedly an appeal, and after a moment Lord Heywood said abruptly:

"I will try to understand, but at the same time you cannot stay here."

"But . . . where can I . . . go?"

"I shall have to consider the answer to that question," he said. "In the meantime, I suggest you get dressed."

As he spoke, he rose to his feet and realised that Lalita was looking at him appraisingly.

"What are you thinking?" he asked.

"I was just wondering whether I would be wiser to refuse to get up until you promise that I can remain here at the Abbey. After all, you could hardly turn me out into the . . . snow with nothing on but my nightgown!"

Lord Heywood laughed.

"If I did," he said, "I have a feeling that by some ingenious and underhanded method of your own you would still get your own way."

She put her head a little on one side as she said:

"In which case can I get up without being afraid?"

"Afraid or not," Lord Heywood said, "the sooner you dress yourself the better! You must realise I should not be sitting here talking to you as you are now."

"There is nobody to be shocked by it except the mice—and there are mice in the wainscotting—but I cannot see that it matters," Lalita answered.

"That is a matter of opinion," Lord Heywood said. "You had better hurry, for if there is any breakfast to be had I shall eat it all, as I am very hungry."

As he spoke he walked to the door, unlocked it, and went out into the passage.

As he did so he heard Lalita give a little cry and he had the idea that she was as hungry as he was.

As he walked down the stairs he thought his return home was certainly different from what he had expected.

He was also aware that finding Lalita had swept away both his mood of depression and his sentimentality, and she had certainly confronted him with a problem to which he had for the moment no solution at all.

* * *

Lalita pushed her empty plate to one side and said:

"Now I feel better! I must admit it was a joy to have toast and butter—two things I have missed these last few days more than I could have believed possible."

Carter had procured eggs and bacon from the Merrivales, some bread which he had toasted, and butter which Lord Heywood learnt they obtained from one of the farms.

"They were very apologetic, M'Lord, that they hadn't more to offer you," Carter said when Lord Heywood found him in the kitchen.

"I am afraid that, little as it may be, we have to share it with somebody else," Lord Heywood replied.

Carter looked at him enquiringly and he explained that he had found there was a lady staying in the house who had hidden herself there when the Merrivales were not looking.

"A sensible thing to do, M'Lord, if 'er didn't want to be found," Carter remarked. "This place's big enough to hide an Army, an' I expects 'er's made 'erself comfortable orl right."

"The question is, what are we going to eat?" Lord Heywood said. "And I hope you have paid the Merrivales for what you have taken from them?"

"I did, but it didn't cost much, M'Lord."

"You will pay the right price," Lord Heywood said

sharply. "Their pension is small enough in all conscience, and it is impossible for me to raise it."

"There's a farm where I 'opes to get somethin' substantial for luncheon, M'Lord, an' if you wants me to pay me way, as you puts it, I'll have to ask you for a few shillin's."

Lord Heywood had taken a guinea from his pocket and put it on the table.

"That, Carter, has to last us for a long time. Buy only what is absolutely essential, and as soon as we have had breakfast I will see what there is in the Gun-Room, which should provide us with a main course if nothing else!"

"We'll not go 'ungry, M'Lord," Carter said cheerfully, "an' I've turned the 'orses into the paddock so's they can fend for 'emselves."

Lord Heywood was gratefully aware that Carter thought of everything.

A quarter-of-an-hour later he thought the same again when he sat down to breakfast in the big Dining-Room at a small table which was covered with a clean white cloth.

The plates were from a dinner-service he had known all his life and were decorated with blue and gold with the Heywood crest emblazoned in the centre of them.

He was just about to eat the eggs and bacon which Carter had brought from the kitchen when Lalita came into the room.

He would have risen to his feet, but she hurried towards him to sit down hastily on a chair.

"Please go on eating," she said. "If you do not know where the next mouthful is coming from, it would be a mistake to let what you already have grow cold."

"Thank you!" Lord Heywood said a little sarcastically.

He told himself that he should resent the intrusion from somebody who had no right to be there.

Instead, he found it difficult not to admit that she was unusually lovely.

She was wearing a thin summer gown which was simply made but was nevertheless, he was sure, an expensive garment.

It was certainly a frame for her slender but exquisitely curved figure, and the ribbons which decorated it were the blue of her eyes.

She had no sooner seated herself than Carter came in carrying a plate of eggs and bacon, which he set down in front of her.

"Mornin', Miss!" he said cheerily. "I 'opes this is to your likin'."

"I am hungry enough to eat a horse!" Lalita replied.

"Not ours, I 'ope!" Carter replied. "Them's the one thing we ain't partin' with!"

"You have horses with you?" Lalita exclaimed. "How wonderful! I am longing to ride. The empty stables look pathetic, like birds' nests after the birds have flown away."

"If you think you are going to ride my horses you are mistaken!" Lord Heywood said sharply.

"Why not?" Lalita asked. "I am a very good rider."

"I am sure you are, but while you stay here, and it must not be for long, you must keep to your original plan of not being seen."

Lalita gave a little laugh.

"You are thinking of your reputation."

"Actually I was thinking of yours," Lord Heywood said, "but now that you mention it, I have no wish to be hailed as a roué the moment I become head of the family!"

"Is your family likely to be calling on you?"

"It might happen, but I hope not. I have nothing to offer them beyond the same fare which you have found monotonous—eggs and vegetables."

"Nonsense!" Lalita said. "You will find lots of things to shoot if you have a good eye."

She looked at him mischievously and added:

"Of course Frenchman are a much bigger target than a bird or a rabbit!"

"I see you are trying to provoke me," Lord Heywood answered, "and I refuse to reply until I have finished eating. As I have already stated, I am extremely hungry!"

Only when they had finished everything on the table and Carter brought nothing more from the kitchen did Lord Heywood say:

"Seriously, Lalita, we will have to make some plans to get you away from here."

"But why can I not stay? I should be very happy with you and your man—what is his name? Carter? He is obviously very efficient and looks after you well, and as I can look after myself, there is no problem."

Lord Heywood gave an exclamation of exasperation.

"Now listen to me, Lalita. I cannot keep repeating myself. You cannot stay here. It would be extremely uncomfortable both for you and for me if it was known that you were here alone and unchaperoned."

"Very well, but where shall I go?"

"You cannot expect me to answer such a stupid question. How do I know?"

"Then it is just as stupid to say that I have to leave. I have told you I could go to France, since if I stay in England there is always the chance that my uncle might find me. Besides, I cannot wander about looking for empty houses, and I know they would think it odd if I tried to put up at an Hotel alone."

Lord Heywood knew they would indeed think it very odd and in most cases would refuse her accommodation.

He supposed there must be some quite easy solution to the problem but for the moment he could not think of it.

"While you are considering whether you should drown me or cut me up into small pieces and bury me in the garden," Lalita said in a small voice, "I would like to go and look at your horses."

"Very well, come and see Waterloo and Conqueror," Lord Heywood conceded.

Lalita gave a cry of delight.

"Is that what you named them after the battle?"

"It was Carter who insisted on it," Lord Heywood replied. "He called his own horse Conqueror and kept on referring to Rollo, as mine had previously been called, as Waterloo, until I accepted that that was now his name."

"I have a feeling, and I shall be disappointed if I am wrong, that he is as magnificent as you are!"

The way she said it did not make it the sort of ingratiating compliment that Lord Heywood had received from the women who pursued him. It was more a statement of fact, and he saw no point in denying it.

Waterloo was certainly very magnificent when they found him in the paddock behind the stables.

Lord Heywood gave his special whistle and the stallion came trotting towards him.

"He is wonderful! Really wonderful!" Lalita exclaimed in delight. "No wonder you love him!"

"How do you know I love him?" Lord Heywood asked.

"You speak to him in a different tone of voice from when you are talking about anything else. And besides, no animal obeys one or comes to the whistle so easily unless he knows he is loved."

Lord Heywood raised his eye-brows but did not comment on what she had said.

He only thought as she stood in her white gown and patted Waterloo that they made a picture which any artist would have wanted to paint.

Lord Heywood knew by the expression in her eyes what she was yearning for, and he found it impossible to resist what he knew she asked for without words.

"I intend to ride Waterloo to visit one or two of the nearer farms," he said. "I expect you would like to accompany me on Conqueror?"

"Can I really do that?"

"Only if when I am at the farms you stay out of sight in the woods near them and the farmers and their wives think I am alone."

"I promise I will, and thank you . . . thank you for saying I may come with you."

"The first thing we have to do is to find you a saddle," Lord Heywood said.

As he spoke, he thought that even if the horses had gone and the stables were empty, there should still be plenty of harness in the Harness-Room.

They went there to find indeed not only bridles and saddles but also harness for carriage-horses which was ornamented with silver and embossed with the Heywood crest.

It struck Lord Heywood that some of it might be saleable, but he reflected that like so many other things this too was likely to be for the moment a glut on the market.

It was only when the horses were saddled and ready that he realised Lalita had not said anything about changing her gown.

"I suppose," he said after a moment, "you have nothing to wear except what you stand up in?"

"Actually I brought two other gowns with me in a valise, and of course my nightgown, but it was heavy enough to make my arm ache before I reached the Stage-Coach."

As she spoke she saw by his expression that she had given Lord Heywood another clue, and she added:

"Stage-Coaches travelling from all directions stop at the top of the village."

"All the same, it took time for you to get here," Lord Heywood said, "which means you might have come from some distance, except that you knew this house was empty and that I was abroad. So your own home must be somewhere in this vicinity."

"Very clever!" Lalita said approvingly. "If I give you one clue everyday, I reckon in about three years' time you will learn who I am and be able to blackmail me by threatening to take me home."

"I should be very ashamed of my intelligence if it takes as long as that!" Lord Heywood replied. "But I suppose it never struck you that if your uncle is making enquiries about you, the guard on your Stage-Coach will be able to tell him where he put you down."

"I thought of that," Lalita said triumphantly, "so I told him I was stopping so as to pick up the fast coach for Oxford. He informed me I had a twenty-minute wait."

She spoke in a manner which showed that she was delighted to have scored a point off her opponent, and Lord Heywood laughed.

"I am beginning to think," he said, "that you are not the poor, pathetic little orphan of the storm you have made yourself out to be, but a very shrewd, experienced trickster!"

"Perhaps I am," Lalita said, "in which case you will have to keep your eye on me, for I shall certainly be able to outwit you if you try to make me do anything I do not wish to do."

Despite himself, Lord Heywood had to admit that he found Lalita amusing, provocative, and certainly very unusual.

He had an idea that she was treating him a little warily, as if she was afraid that she might after all be unable to persuade him to let her stay.

At the same time, he knew that it was becoming more and more difficult to decide what was the right course he should take.

It was certainly reprehensible that she should be staying alone with him in an empty house, but he could not conjure up a Chaperone from nowhere, and he was also too beset by his own problems to have time to concentrate fully on Lalita's.

His visit to the first farm was horrifying.

The farmer was getting old, one of his sons had joined the Army, and another had been press-ganged into the Navy. The third was little more than a child, trying to help his father with the assistance of what Lord Heywood privately thought must be the "village idiot."

The cows were too old to give much milk and the pigs had not enough food to fatten them for market. There were an exceptional number of scraggy hens, but there was no other livestock.

Very little of the ground had been ploughed, and what had been had produced a crop of weeds and nettles.

"Surely you obtained good prices for what you could sell in the war?" Lord Heywood asked.

"That were true, M'Lord, but 'tweren't easy to grow

much when us were short-'anded, and th' last three years things 'ave been bad, very bad!"

Lord Heywood knew they looked to him hopefully to repair and restock the farm, but while he told them cautiously that he had a lot to do first, he could not bear to inform them bluntly that as far as he was concerned the future seemed hopeless.

He found the same conditions at the next farm, which depressed him so much that he decided that would be enough for one day and rode home.

He was so deep in thought that he almost forgot Lalita's existence until she said:

"You will have to do something for them, and for yourself."

"I have not the least idea what!" Lord Heywood answered sharply.

"But something must be done."

"Only a miracle can be of any use, and that should come in the form of golden guineas, like manna from Heaven."

"Miracles do happen!"

"In the past, in the Bible, and in fairy-stories," Lord Heywood said. "We have to face reality, Lalita."

" 'God helps those who help themselves.' "

"I am only too willing to help myself if somebody will show me how," Lord Heywood replied bitterly.

The Abbey looked so magnificent that it seemed impossible to believe that with all its contents he still had not a penny to spend on it.

As if Lalita read his thoughts she said:

"Have you got a list of the contents?"

"Yes, of course."

"Well, suppose they made a mistake and you find that they have not listed everything?"

41

"My Solicitor assures me they did the job thoroughly."

"Perhaps there is some treasure hidden under the floor-boards or in the cellars."

"If I find some bottles of wine in the latter, I will see if there is one we can enjoy for our dinner."

"As you say that, I imagine I am welcome to stay with you tonight, at any rate," Lalita said demurely.

"I suppose so," he admitted, "but I would like to add that you must pack up and leave tomorrow morning."

"I cannot believe you would have enjoyed your ride half so much with Carter as you did with me."

Because it was the truth, it irritated him.

"I can assure you," he said, "I have every intention of thinking of somewhere you can go, but for the moment my own difficulties come first."

"But of course, and that is why I want to help you."

"There is nothing you can do."

"Do not be too sure of that. I am a Celt—there is another clue for you—and all Celts have special powers. My mother was a water-diviner when she wished to be."

"We have plenty of water, thank you," Lord Heywood said, looking at the lake.

"I have a feeling that one day I shall surprise you," Lalita said.

"You have done that already," he remarked. "How could I imagine when I arrived home this morning that I would find a stowaway in my mother's bedroom?"

Lalita gave a cry of laughter.

"That is exactly what I am—a stowaway! And no humane Captain would throw me overboard."

"I think that is a popular illusion," Lord Heywood said. "And let me point out that stowaways have to work their passage."

"I have every intention of doing so," Lalita replied, "and when you find I am indispensable, you will then be grateful to me for choosing your ship in which to hide myself."

She spoke with a sincerity which he found rather amusing.

Then as he watched her ride the large charger ahead of him through the gateway into the stable, looking very lovely in her white gown with the blue ribbons, he thought that none of his friends, if they were told of it, would believe what was happening to him.

Chapter Three

"Lalita!"

Lord Heywood called as he walked into the Hall.

"I am here!"

He heard her voice from the Writing-Room, and even as he moved towards the sound she came running through the door towards him.

"You are back!" she exclaimed unnecessarily. "What happened?"

Lalita knew even as she spoke that the answer would not be a pleasant one, and Lord Heywood, without replying, walked past her and into the room she had just left.

The Writing-Room, which was a rather prosaic name for the exquisitely designed Salon which opened out of the huge Library, was the room he had decided to use.

There was such a large choice in the vast house that it had been a difficult decision until Lalita pointed out that he would need a desk and there was a very attractive one, made two centuries earlier, in the Writing-Room.

Decorated with white walls picked out in gold and with a huge chandelier hanging from the ceiling, it actually looked more suitable for a party than as a Sitting-Room for everyday use.

But the chairs and sofas were comfortable and there were also a number of books which Lalita had been dusting.

Some of them were scattered on the floor and her hands and the duster showed how dirty they had become from the neglect of several years.

Lalita was also aware, as Lord Heywood walked across the room to stand with his back to the empty fireplace, that she herself was looking very strange.

She was wearing a housemaid's apron which was too large for her over her gown, and she had covered her head with a small square of linen, which she now hurriedly removed.

The sunshine coming through the window lit up the gold of her hair and when she pushed it back from her forehead she left a smudge of dust on her white skin.

Lord Heywood, however, was not concerned with Lalita's appearance and she knew by the frown between his eyes and the squareness of his chin that he was upset.

When he had left her after breakfast he had told her that he was going to visit the pensioners on the Estate, and she had thought apprehensively that it would not be entirely a pleasant visit or a happy reunion with the old people he had known before he had gone abroad.

"What did you find?" she asked softly.

"Of the fifteen cottages I visited," he replied, "thirteen need urgent repairs done to them."

"I was afraid of that."

"The roofs leak, the floor-boards have given way, the chimneys smoke, and God knows what else is wrong!"

There was silence. Then as if Lalita sensed that he had not told her the whole story she asked:

"What else?"

"They are expecting their pensions at the end of the week, which will be the first of the month, and I have no idea if Crosswaith, my Solicitor, intends to pay them and increase the large amount of money I owe them already."

There was a note in Lord Heywood's voice which told Lalita what he was feeling more effectively than if he had put it into words.

"What will you do?" she asked.

"I must go to London tomorrow and see them," he replied. "I must also sell the few things that are not in trust and hope that when that money is spent, something else will turn up."

There was silence. Then Lalita said:

"We have not nearly finished going round the house to see if there is anything else which can be sold."

"The only things here which are mine personally belonged to my mother."

Lalita gave a little cry.

"I cannot bear you to part with the paintings in her bedroom or that chest which you told me had been in her family for centuries before she married your father."

"It is no use being sentimental," Lord Heywood replied in a harsh voice.

Once again there was silence before Lalita said:

"Do you think there is . . . anything in . . . London that the Solicitors have not . . . listed?"

"That is what I intend to find out. I am also determined to put the house on the market, not for sale—I am not allowed to do that—but perhaps somebody may rent it from me."

He knew as he spoke that it was a forlorn hope and Lalita knew the same.

Before coming to the Abbey she had heard of quite a number of people who were either closing up or trying to let their London houses, finding it difficult enough to keep up one dwelling-house, let alone two.

Now she looked appealingly at Lord Heywood before she said hesitantly:

"I . . . I have some . . . jewellery with me which . . . belonged to my . . . mother. I was going to . . . suggest that you sell it for me . . . anyway . . . but I s-suppose you would not consider . . . borrowing the proceeds until such time as I . . . need them?"

For a moment Lord Heywood's thoughts were diverted from his trouble on the Estate and he looked at Lalita as if he was really seeing her for the first time since he had come back to the house.

She thought he would snap at her, but he smiled.

"I appreciate that you are trying to find a solution to my problems," he said, "but, my dear girl, you should be thinking of your own. Believe me, you will need every penny you possess, unless you intend to return home."

"You know I cannot do that," Lalita answered, "but if I do not . . . leave you, then I do not . . . need the money."

"Now we are back where we started," Lord Heywood said, "and you know my opinions on that subject."

"Only too well!" Lalita replied. "But if you had any common sense you would realise my suggestion is a practical one."

"It is very impractical and, as you are aware, I may be poor, but I still have my pride."

"Pride comes before a fall sooner or later."

Lord Heywood walked across the room to stand looking out the window and Lalita knew he was asking himself what he could do about the people who were dependent upon him and who with the rapidly rising prices after the war could hardly manage to survive on their meagre pensions.

There were admittedly Workhouses of some sort in the County, perhaps several, but they were places from which the poor shrank, and the stories of the way the inmates were treated had been a subject of constant criticism before Lord Heywood had left the country.

He asked himself how could he let the old men and women who had worked for his father and his grandfather until they no longer had the strength to do any more, end their remaining years in such conditions.

"I have to find some money," he said beneath his breath.

"Supposing you did sell one of the paintings which are entailed," Lalita asked, "and perhaps some of the china. What would happen?"

"As soon as it was discovered, as it would be sooner or later," Lord Heywood replied without turning round, "the Trustees would take me before the Magistrates and I should be told I was more or less a thief. The scandal would be extremely unpleasant."

Lalita gave a sigh.

She knew how much this would hurt him and he was too honourable and too upright to do such a thing.

"You must be able to find something that would bring in a little money," she said despondently.

"A little would not be enough," Lord Heywood retorted. "But as I have said, I will go to London tomorrow."

As if he could not bear to talk of it any longer he walked out of the room, and Lalita put her hand up to her forehead in an effort to think, forgetting how dirty it was.

For the three days that she had been at the Abbey since Lord Heywood had come home she had felt as if the problem of money encroached more menacingly on them every day.

She had taken the large Inventory which Lord Heywood had obtained from Mr. Crosswaith and had gone round a number of the rooms looking to see if anything had been overlooked, only to find that there was practically nothing that had not been included.

"How can your grandfather have been so tiresome," she asked, "as to entail all this in such detail?"

"My grandfather and my great-grandfather were great collectors," Lord Heywood replied. "I think my father rather frightened them when he was a young man."

He was aware that Lalita was waiting for an explanation and went on:

"At Oxford he was very wild and, in their opinion, an inveterate spendthrift."

"So they were afraid he might sell the things they had collected?"

Lord Heywood nodded.

"When he was sent down from the University he went to London, where his Curricules, his Phaetons, and his horses were the joy of the caricaturists. He also managed in two years to lose a considerable fortune at the card-tables."

"I can understand your grandfather thinking that he was not to be trusted with all the treasures here."

"My grandfather paid up for him dozens of times and lectured him day in and day out, but he continued to be extravagant until his dying day."

Lord Heywood's voice sharpened as he added:

"That is why I am in the position I am in now."

"But you can still live in a magnificent house filled with treasures."

"And starve as I do so! Not a very pleasant prospect."

"You would find it more unpleasant to have to live in a cottage or sleep under the trees."

Lord Heywood smiled.

"I expect I could find an empty house belonging to somebody else!"

Lalita's eyes twinkled.

"You have to admit it was clever of me to come here. If you had not come home, nobody would have been any the wiser."

"You could hardly have stayed here for years talking only to the mice."

"That is what I thought I would have to do until you appeared unexpectedly in my bedroom. It was a considerable shock!"

"It was a shock for me too!" Lord Heywood said.

All the same, Lalita was intuitive enough to realise that because she was there he was not finding his problem as depressing as he might have done otherwise, and Carter confirmed this.

"If you asks me," he said when Lalita was talking to him in the kitchen, "it's a good thing the Colonel 'as you to grumble to, so to speak."

"I thought that myself," Lalita replied.

"Seems stupid-like t' me," Carter went on. " 'Ere's this house filled with gold, so to speak, an' none o' us dares put a finger on it!"

"It is very frustrating for His Lordship, but he is worrying not about himself but about the people who are dependent upon him."

"That's 'im all over," Carter agreed. "There weren't an Officer like 'im in the Regiment. Looked after 'is men, 'e did, with never a thought for 'imself, an' there weren't nothin' they wouldn't do for 'im!"

"That is how you feel, is it not, Carter?" Lalita asked.

Yesterday when Lord Heywood was out she had gone to the kitchen and found that Carter was just about to walk up to the nearest farm to buy them some food.

She saw him counting the money which he had taken from a drawer in the kitchen, and she said:

"Carter, if I suggest something to you, will you promise not to tell His Lordship?"

"Depends what it is, Miss," Carter replied.

"When I ran away," Lalita said, "I took quite a lot of money with me because I was not so foolish as to think I could manage without it."

She saw that Carter was listening attentively and went on:

"I told His Lordship I would pay my way, but of course he refused, as I am a woman. Yet even women have to eat, and eating has to be paid for."

"I'm not goin' to argue with that," Carter said.

"That is why," Lalita went on, "I intend to pay my way without His Lordship knowing about it."

She thought Carter was about to refuse and she said quickly:

"It is a case of either I go out and buy some food, which would be dangerous because then people will know I am here, or you buy it for me."

" 'Is Lordship'll skin me alive if 'e gets to 'ear o' it."

"Then we must be clever and not let him know," Lalita said.

She put three sovereigns down on the kitchen-table.

"When you have spent that I will give you some more. I think it important that His Lordship is properly fed and I am quite sure that meat is expensive."

Carter was looking at the sovereigns and there was a glint in his eyes.

"Please say nothing to His Lordship," Lalita insisted. "He is a strong man, but he takes a lot out of himself. You know as well as I do that like Waterloo and Conqueror he needs proper feeding."

"I were a-thinkin' I could steal some oats for them 'orses," Carter said, "but they at th' farms be as poor as us."

"Most farmers are in the same state all over the country," Lalita replied. "But as His Lordship said, we have to pay our way, and that is what I intend we shall do, and as I have money it is not really difficult."

Swiftly, as if he felt he must do it surreptitiously, Carter swept up the sovereigns and slipped them into his pocket.

"Gawd 'elp me if 'is Lordship finds out!" he said. "But if 'e does I shall tell 'im as 'twas Eve as tempted me!"

"The age-old excuse of every man!" Lalita laughed.

At the same time, she was delighted to have got her own way.

She knew that Lord Heywood, like most men, would accept food when it was there and not ask too many questions as to what it had cost, and she was right.

At dinner last evening Lord Heywood had eaten several slices of a prime sirloin of beef and merely said when he had finished:

"That was excellent, Carter! I always said you were the best cook in the Regiment. I was afraid they would take you from me to cook for the Officers' Mess."

"I'd soon 'ave got out o' there, M'Lord," Carter said. "Two meals'd be enough with what I'd serve them up!"

Lord Heywood laughed.

"I know how your mind works! At the same time,

Miss Lalita and I would like to thank you for being so proficient. The beef was delicious!"

Carter had removed what was left from the table and as he did so he winked at Lalita.

She thought it was somewhat reprehensible behaviour on the part of Lord Heywood's man-servant. At the same time, she thought that good food downed with a bottle of wine from the cellar had put His Lordship in a mellow mood.

He had sat in the Writing-Room after dinner, not talking of how she must leave but instead planning how they could make it more comfortable with extra chairs and cushions from the Salons.

He had even been ready to exchange one of the paintings for one that Lalita particularly liked in a room that they had no intention of using.

"Tomorrow I am going to choose some different ornaments for the mantelshelf," she said, "and bring in some of those exquisite pieces of Dresden china from the Grand Salon to stand on the gilt table in the corner."

He did not protest but merely smiled at her indulgently, and she thought once again that his agreeable mood was due to the fact that he felt well fed.

"I have something to ask you," she said at breakfast the next day.

"What is it?"

Lord Heywood asked the question but he was in fact reading the newspaper as he ate his eggs and bacon.

It was a day old, but Carter had brought it from the village, and Lord Heywood realised how out-of-touch he was with all the current news both political and social.

"You know, because I told you so," Lalita said in a small voice, "that I was only able to bring three gowns

53

away with me—two in the valise I carried and the one I was wearing?"

"Yes, you told me that," Lord Heywood answered vaguely.

"I was wondering if you would . . . think it very wrong and . . . perhaps almost . . . insulting if I asked you if I could wear your . . . mother's riding-habit."

She spoke hesitatingly, and now Lord Heywood raised his head to look at her in surprise.

"My mother's riding-habit?" he questioned.

"There are a lot of her clothes in the wardrobe of the bedroom where I am sleeping."

"I never thought of it, but I suppose there would be," Lord Heywood said, "just as I have been thinking that not only the clothes I left behind fortunately still fit me but also my father's."

"You . . you may dislike my wearing your mother's . . . clothes," Lalita said, "but it does not . . . improve my own to ride in them."

"I can appreciate that," Lord Heywood remarked. "And I imagine that your gowns may have to last you for a long time."

He smiled before he added:

"Take anything of my mother's you like. I have a feeling that if she knew what was happening it would amuse her."

He saw Lalita's eyes light up.

"Thank you, thank you!" she cried. "And it is strange you should say that! Sleeping in her bedroom I sometimes feel as if she is there, and she is not in the least disapproving because I have run away, as you try to be!"

"That is something you cannot prove," Lord Heywood said, "but I imagine you wish to come riding with me, in which case you had better go and change."

"I will be very quick!" Lalita promised, and she sped from the Dining-Room as if there were wings on her heels.

Lord Heywood had to admit to himself that she amused him.

There was never a moment in the day when he did not find she had something unusual and invariably intelligent to say, and she certainly kept him from feeling as depressed and despondent about the future as he would have been otherwise.

She had set herself the task of cleaning the rooms which they used.

House-work was something he was sure she had never done before, but the manner in which she applied herself to the task was very commendable.

He was well aware that the ladies who pursued him in Paris and those he remembered at home in the past would never have demeaned themselves by doing anything so unpleasant as brushing and dusting.

While Carter swept the worst of the dust off the carpets, Lalita brushed down the furniture and dusted the ornaments, the tables, and the mirrors.

Lord Heywood found that his bed was made up with the best sheets, which he was sure was Lalita's doing, and every day the furniture, dusted and polished, looked more as it had when he was a boy.

It was obviously impossible for them to tackle the whole of the house, but Lalita polished the bannister so that they did not get their hands dirty when they touched it, and Carter cleaned the Dining-Room until everything shone in the sunlight.

Even so, Lord Heywood could not help remembering the six tall footmen dressed in the family livery of green and yellow who stood in the Hall in the past, and how impressive old Merrivale had looked, before he shrunk with old age, when he had received their guests with almost pontifical dignity.

There had been half-a-dozen housemaids in their mob-caps bustling in and out of the bedrooms, and a House-keeper in rustling black taffeta and with a silver chate-laine at her waist, supervising everything with an eagle eye.

Now as he saw Lalita look a little ruefully at her hands he felt guilty.

"There is no need for you to do this," he said sharply an hour later when he came back into the Writing-Room to find her still dusting books.

"We cannot get as black as a chimney-sweep every time we take a book from the shelves," she replied. "Besides, they deteriorate if they are not looked after."

"There is no need for you to worry about them," he said without thinking.

Lalita sat back on her heels and looked up at him.

"Are you feeling disagreeable?" she asked. "Because I was going to suggest that you might like to do some work in the Peach-House."

"The Peach-House?" Lord Heywood exclaimed.

"I know you have not had much time to look at the kitchen-garden," Lalita went on, "but the peaches are beginning to ripen, and Carter thinks the nectarines should be ready to eat in another week. Also, if you are very good you shall have strawberries for dinner!"

Lord Heywood laughed.

"You are making me feel as if I had just come back from School and all those things are a special treat."

"That is exactly what they are," Lalita said, "but of course if you are unkind, I shall punish you by eating them all myself."

Lord Heywood laughed again.

"Carter has said that luncheon will be ready in exactly five minutes, and you know how punctual he is. It will take you all that time to get your hands clean."

"Whether they are clean or not, I am very hungry!" Lalita said.

Jumping up from the floor and holding up her apron so that she could move quicker, she ran from the room.

Lord Heywood watched her go and thought to himself that she was an amusing child, and although he admitted that he liked having her here, he knew he should definitely make plans for her to leave.

'As soon as I come back from London I must do something about it,' he thought.

He was sure that it was only a question of time before various of his acquaintances in the County would be aware that he was home and would call out of curiosity if nothing else.

He could not imagine anything more disastrous than for them to find that he had a young, unchaperoned woman staying with him and he did not even know her name.

"She will have to leave," Lord Heywood decided.

But he had no idea how he could persuade her to go or where he could send her.

He found himself every night puzzling over who she could be and how it had been possible for her to disappear in such a strange manner without there being a hue and cry.

He almost expected to find a description of her in the newspapers.

He had decided, from what she had said and her knowledge of the Abbey and the conditions surrounding it, that she must live somewhere locally.

He could of course ask Carter to make enquiries at the village Inn or at the farms as to whether they had heard of anybody missing in the vicinity.

Then he told himself that that would be unfair. Lalita trusted him and he could not betray that trust by taking any action that might jeopardise her freedom.

Nevertheless, what would happen to her?

She was far too young and too beautiful to move about the world alone, and it made him shudder to think of the dangers she would encounter.

He was still thinking of Lalita when she came back, looking very much cleaner and without the housemaid's apron which had protected her gown.

He noticed, although he did not say so, that her small hands were distinctly pink and he knew it must have been from the way she had to scrub them to get rid of the dirt and dust.

Her skin was white and translucent as a pearl, and he thought again how lovely she was and how ill-equipped to be alone in what would undoubtedly be a hostile and frightening world.

As they walked towards the Dining-Room, Lord Heywood wondered how many men of his acquaintance would have behaved as he was doing in the same circumstances or how many women would make no effort to attract him physically.

There were few women in the same position who would not have flirted with him and tried to entice him. But Lalita was provocative only in a mischievous and amusing manner.

He supposed it was her age and her innocence which prevented her from regarding him as a man.

He knew, because she had told him, that she thought he was handsome and magnificent, and she deferred to his judgement, which in itself was a subtle form of flattery.

But it was very different from the blandishments and the amatory indiscretions which Lord Heywood had previously found were inevitable when he was alone with a woman.

He found himself thinking of Lady Irene and knowing how very different everything would have been if she had been alone here with him at the Abbey.

Lady Irene Dawlish had made it very clear when he was in Paris what her feelings were towards him. But although he had found her exceedingly attractive and she had provided for him a fiery interlude in the midst of his other duties, he had not been sorry to say goodbye to her when he left for England.

Her husband had been killed in action and buried in France, so she had come out from England to see his grave after hostilities had ended.

It was the Duke of Wellington who had introduced them, Lady Irene being a distant cousin of the Duchess, and Lord Heywood had more or less been told to look after her and prevent her visit from being entirely a sorrowful one.

He had soon learnt that Lady Irene was in fact not as broken-hearted over her husband's death as might have been expected.

She had married when she was very young but had soon regretted her impetuosity. She therefore had not found it a hardship to find herself widowed with enough money to live in comfort and be acclaimed as one of the most beautiful women in the *Beau Monde*.

The Duke of Wellington, who always had an eye for a pretty woman, undoubtedly would have looked after her himself if he had not been heavily engaged with another charmer who was extremely jealous and very possessive.

He therefore left it to Lord Heywood to show Lady Irene the delights of Paris, to escort her to the graveside of her husband, then back again to the gaieties of the French Capital.

Lady Irene had been very satisfied with the escort chosen for her by the Duke.

She lost no time in making Lord Heywood aware that the only way she could be quickly consoled for the loss of her husband and amused by Paris was to be in his arms.

It had been a long time since he had had any female companionship, except of the more sordid nature, and now that there was no fighting to be done he had time on his hands.

Lord Heywood would not have been human if he had not accepted what the fates offered.

However, as time passed he had become uneasily aware that Lady Irene was asking more from him than a fiery interlude in a busy life, which was all she meant to him.

Although she was promiscuous in her *affaires de coeur* and in her mind regarded every man who approached her as a potential lover, Lady Irene also wished to marry again.

When she learnt that the man she knew as "Colonel Romney Wood" was in fact Lord Heywood, she decided that she was willing to become his wife.

She was aware that he had little money, but that was immaterial beside the fact that he owned one of the finest and most magnificent houses in England.

Lady Irene could see herself entertaining there and at Heywood House in London, which was considerably larger and more impressive than the house she had been left by Dawlish.

"I love you, Romney!" she had said the night before Lord Heywood left Paris. "As soon as I come back to London we must make plans for our future."

It was the first time she had said anything so direct, although she had hinted that she wanted them to be together for life, but Lord Heywood had said nothing.

"I have never loved anybody as I love you!" Lady Irene continued, moving closer, if it was possible, and putting her arm round his neck to pull his head down to hers.

"We will be very, very happy together, and, darling, no woman ever had a more ardent or demanding lover!"

Her lips, fierce and hungry, swept away any reply that Lord Heywood might have made.

While his body found it impossible not to respond to the fire she ignited in him, his mind told him firmly and dispassionately that he had no intention of marrying Lady Irene or anybody like her.

He did not know what sort of wife he wanted, but he was quite certain that for many years yet he would avoid taking one.

However, if he had to marry, then it would certainly not be a woman who he suspected as soon as he left Paris would console herself with one of his brother-officers or one of the young diplomats who were only too delighted to become involved in a tempestuous if short-lived love-affair.

As he and Lalita entered the Dining-Room they saw Carter come hurrying from the kitchen-entrance with a steaming dish in his hands, and Lord Heywood thought that money or no money, he would much rather be here with Lalita than with Lady Irene.

They rode after luncheon until they thought the horses had had enough for one day, then came back to explore the kitchen-garden, as Lalita had suggested.

Lord Heywood saw that the peaches, having been left to grow wild, were not nearly as large as he remembered them being, although the trees were laden with them.

The grapes were ripening too and he cut down a bunch for Lalita and she ate them appreciatively while they went on to explore the greenhouses.

The orchids had suffered through neglect but they were still blooming, while the carnations made her cry out with delight, and she picked a large bunch to carry back to the house.

"There is far too much fruit here for us to eat it all," she said. "I will tell you what I will do with some of the peaches: I will make you the most delicious fruit-drink which Mama used to make for me when I was a little girl. It was something she learnt when she was a child in Boston."

She saw Lord Heywood look at her sharply and she gave a rueful little smile as she said:

"That is undoubtedly your clue for today."

"So your mother was American!"

"I suppose after that slip it would be stupid for me to lie or to refuse to answer."

"Very stupid!" Lord Heywood agreed. "And gradually, like a puzzle, I am fitting into place what I learn from you. Soon you will be obliged to tell me the whole story."

"But think how disappointing it will be for you when you have nothing else to think about," Lalita replied.

"Nothing else!" he exclaimed. Then laughed. "You cannot side-track me so easily!"

"I would like to . . . tell you everything," Lalita said, "but I think it would be . . . a mistake."

"From your point of view or mine?"

"Really, from yours," she answered. "You see, if you knew everything about me, then you might feel it your duty to find my Guardian and take me back to him. As

it is, you can salve your conscience . . . if you have one
. . . by saying that I kept you in ignorance and therefore there was nothing you could do but act like a Good
Samaritan."

Lord Heywood knew this was very near the truth, so
he asked no more questions.

Lalita had admitted she had jewellery with her and
money, and he knew that if she wandered about the
country alone, sooner or later she would be robbed and
perhaps injured in the process.

He had noticed the newspaper reports of the trouble
that had been caused by men who had disbanded from
the Army and the Navy without pensions, and having
quickly spent what they had, they were roaming about
the country either begging, stealing, or robbing travellers.

It frightened him to think of what dangers Lalita
would encounter in such circumstances, and he was
well aware that she had no idea, having always been
looked after and cosseted, what life could be like if she
was alone and unprotected.

As if she followed the train of his thoughts, Lalita
slipped her hand into his.

"I am very grateful . . . very, very grateful," she
said, "and sometimes I think Mama, who believed in
prayer, guided me here and brought you home at just
the right moment to look after me."

Lord Heywood wanted to reply that he thought that
was too fanciful and impossible to substantiate.

But there was something very young and confiding in
the way Lalita spoke, and he thought her fingers in his
were those of a trusting child.

So, instead of the words which trembled on his lips,
he said:

"I should like to drink your peach-juice, which is
something I have never tasted before."

*   *   *

Before dinner that night Lord Heywood told Carter that he intended to go to London the next day.

"How's Your Lordship a-travellin'?"

"I thought I would ride Waterloo."

"There's a nice Curricle in th' stables, an' it can't be very old as I sees it's an up-to-date model."

"A Curricle?"

"Your Lordship can 'ave Conqueror. Waterloo wouldn't stand for it, but there be a young horse th' farmers been a-driving with a gig, which'd make a pair."

"It would certainly be a better way to travel to London," Lord Heywood mused.

"I'll go up to th' farm an' borrow th' 'orse, M'Lord. Give 'em a good rest when Your Lordship gets there an' plenty o' oats an' they'll bring yer back safe and sound th' next day."

"You are right, Carter. It would certainly be more comfortable and I should not have to change when I reach London."

Although Conqueror was a far better bred animal, the young horse from the farm obviously had stamina and they were not badly matched.

The Curricle was painted black and yellow and Lord Heywood thought it was very smart. It would be comfortable to drive, and he looked forward to the journey with pleasure.

He was aware as he put on his tall hat that Lalita was staring at him in admiration.

She had in fact been surprised when she came down to breakfast to find him dressed in a way which she had never seen before.

As he had previously worn only riding-breeches and a comfortable riding-coat with a cravat tied loosely round his throat, she had not expected him to be wearing clothes that would have adorned any Buck or Beau in St. James's.

His tight-fitting knitted champagne-coloured pantaloons that had been introduced by the Prince Regent were worn with highly polished Hessians in which Carter had said proudly "yer can see yer face if yer want to."

The cut-away coat with its long tails had, Lalita knew, originally been introduced by Beau Brummell, and Lord Heywood's cravat was tied in a Mathematical Style which was always described in the newspapers as being the most complicated of those favoured by the Dandies.

She stared at him wide-eyed and Lord Heywood smiled a little self-consciously before he said:

"I never expected that the clothes I wore when I was young and foolish would have survived for so long!"

"They fit you perfectly!"

"Too perfectly!" he replied. "I think life in the Army has enlarged my muscles, so my coat, I may tell you confidentially, is uncomfortably tight!"

"But you look marvellous! What I have always heard described as a very 'Tulip of Fashion'!"

"Thank you," Lord Heywood laughed. "It is something I do not aspire to be, but it was either these clothes or the ones you have seen me wearing up until now."

"You would have been ashamed to appear in London in those!"

"Perhaps you are right," he said, "and Banks do not give credit to those who look impoverished."

"Is that where you are going?"

"I intend to try to obtain a loan, but I am not particularly optimistic that I shall succeed."

"I am sure they will understand your circumstances,"

Lalita said, "and while you are away I will pray very, very hard that they will be accommodating."

"I am sure your prayers will help me," Lord Heywood replied, "and now I had better be on my way."

Lalita walked with him to the front door, feeling, although it was absurd, somewhat forlorn because she could not go with him and had to be left behind.

"I will look after the house until you come back," she said.

"I thought it was looking after you!" Lord Heywood replied.

"Carter will do . . . that."

"And I hope neither of you will get into any trouble in any way."

"We will not," Lalita promised, "but . . . please hurry . . . back."

There was no doubt it was a plea, and for the moment he was rather touched that she would so obviously miss him.

"I will be as quick as I can," he said, "but if I am not back tomorrow night, do not worry."

"That is very easy to say," Lalita protested, "but I shall worry, so . . . please try not to . . . waste the delicious meal we will have . . . waiting for you."

Lord Heywood smiled at her, and as she lifted her face to look up at him pleadingly he had the strange idea that he should kiss her good-bye.

Then quickly he stepped into the Curricle, picked up the reins, and drove off.

As he looked back he thought that Lalita, standing on the steps with the great house behind her, looked woebegone but very lovely.

It was strange, but she seemed to belong there, almost as if the house itself framed and protected her.

Chapter Four

As the horses disappeared out of sight Lalita turned and walked into the house, saying to Carter as she did so:

"I do hope he will be all right."

" 'Is Lordship can drive anything," Carter replied, "even a mule an' a donkey if you put 'em together."

Lalita laughed, then at that moment she heard somebody behind them.

She looked back and saw that the postman had come round the house from the direction of the back-door.

He walked up the steps and thrust two letters into Carter's hands.

"Oi've been a-knockin' me head off at th' back," he said, "an' not a sight nor sound o' anyone!"

"Th' sixth footman must be a-lyin' down!" Carter retorted.

Lalita did not wait to hear this exchange of wit but walked into the Hall.

When Carter joined her a second or so later she said:

"I wonder if the letters are important. It is a pity His Lordship could . . . not have had them before he left."

"One looks to I to be a bill," Carter said, inspecting the letters in his hand, "an' there ain't no 'urry for th' other."

"How do you know that?" Lalita enquired.

" 'Cos it's from someun 'is Lordship was real glad to leave behind when we left Paris."

Lalita knew this must have been a woman and she could not help feeling curious.

"Was she very . . . beautiful?" she asked, then was ashamed of herself for being so inquisitive.

"Who? Lidy Irene?" Carter enquired.

"Was that her name?"

"That's right. Lidy Irene Dawlish, an' the person who admired 'er the most were 'erself!"

Carter spoke in a contemptuous tone which Lalita knew was impertinent.

At the same time she was interested.

"I . . . suppose," she said hesitatingly after a moment, "because His Lordship is so . . . handsome there are always lots of ladies to tell him so."

"Yer bet! After 'im like flies round a 'oney-pot, they was," Carter replied. "Always askin' my 'elp too."

Lalita looked puzzled and he explained, mimicking a woman's voice:

" 'Carter, what time can I see 'is Lordship alone?' or, 'Carter, will you tell 'im I am waiting and I 'ave something very important to say to 'im.' "

Carter laughed derisively.

" 'Twas important orl right—to them!"

Lalita said nothing but she found herself thinking of Lord Heywood in a new light.

It was perhaps his appearance when he had driven off to London looking so smart and so dashing that made her think that neither her father nor his friends would have been able to compete with him.

He was a lot younger than they had been and very much better-looking.

But there was something more about him which she had never noticed in any other man.

Now she wondered if he had gone to London not only to see his Solicitors, as he had told her, but if his visit would include meeting some beautiful lady like the one who had written to him.

She had seen the hand-writing on the letter which Carter had put down on a table at the bottom of the stairs, and she noted it was very flowery and in a way flamboyant.

Lalita found herself conjuring up a picture of the sort of lady who would be attracted to Lord Heywood and he to her.

"I wonder why His Lordship has never married," she said aloud.

"Married?" Carter exclaimed. "That's somethin' 'e's never thought about while I've been with 'im, an' it's nothin' 'e can afford."

"He could marry a rich wife."

"And 'ave a woman hold th' purse-strings an' order 'im about?" Carter enquired. "Not 'is Lordship! But I'm not saying 'e 'asn't 'ad 'is chances."

Carter glanced at the letter on the table as he spoke, and as if she knew what he was thinking Lalita said:

"I suppose Lady Irene had money."

"So I 'ears," Carter answered cautiously.

"Then if His Lordship married her he would be able to restore this house to its former glory. There would be servants and gardeners, horses in the stables, and he would not have to worry over the farmers and the pensioners."

"If you ask me, them worries wouldn't count beside those Lady Irene'd bring 'im."

"I gather you did not like her?"

"Like 'er?" Carter repeated. " 'Er's th' sort I wouldn't trust on a dark night wi' a blind man!"

Then, as if he suddenly realised to whom he was speaking, he added quickly:

"It's not th' sort o' thing, Miss, I should be a-sayin' to you, an' I've some washing-up to do."

He walked off swiftly towards the kitchen, but Lalita was looking serious as she went towards the Writing-Room.

When she saw the newspapers from the day before lying untidily on the floor and an empty glass that Lord Heywood had brought from the Dining-Room, it struck her that the place was empty and lonely without him.

She began to tidy the room, at the same time thinking how unexpectedly happy she had been the last few days.

She had never known before what it was like to be alone with a young man whom she could talk to, squabble with, and tease.

She had been happy with her grandfather after her father and mother died, but he was old and used to always having his own way, so he seldom listened to her opinions.

Now she thought it had been very exciting to be able to express herself, to be aware that Lord Heywood was listening, and also to try to defeat him in an argument.

They had discussed many subjects when they were not going over his problems or she was putting obstacles in his way when he tried to find out more about her.

Even that was exciting, knowing that she was staying

on in his house simply because he was too decent and too much of a gentleman to turn her out.

"He seems to like having me here," Lalita told herself.

Then she wondered if he would have preferred to have somebody like Lady Irene, who loved him and to whom he could "make love."

She was not certain what that implied, but she had the idea that it might be very exciting to be made love to by Lord Heywood.

This inevitably made her remember her cousin whom her uncle had tried to make her marry.

Because the thought of him was so horrifying and in a way disgusting, she hurriedly picked up the glass and carried it to the kitchen so that she could talk to Carter and not be alone with her thoughts.

He was busy skinning a rabbit.

"Did you catch that in one of your snares?" she asked.

"This be th' second rabbit I've caught in that 'un," Carter replied.

"Poor little thing!" Lalita said. "I feel it is rather cruel to catch them unawares, but at the same time there are so many of them, and we are hungry."

" 'Tis no use yer worryin' 'bout rabbits, Miss," Carter replied. "It's 'is Lordship you and me 'ave to think about."

'As if I could think of anybody else!' Lalita thought, and remembered that she had promised to pray that he would be successful in obtaining a loan from the Bank.

*　　*　　*

Lord Heywood reached London without much trouble with his horses.

After they had settled down to a comfortable pace he had been able to think of a plan of action once he

71

reached his destination and especially how he should approach the Bank.

He had calculated that he should be at Heywood House by about twelve o'clock, and when he arrived he put the horses in the empty stable in the Mews and managed, by tipping a groom of an adjacent stable, to procure some oats for them.

He then went round to the front-door of Heywood House and rang the bell.

He could hear it clanging away in the distance, and he took several more pulls at it and also used the knocker before finally the door was opened by a very old and bowed man.

It took Lord Heywood a second or two to recognise Johnson, who was the Butler and whom he had not seen for many years.

Johnson was not only deaf but going blind, and it took some time for Lord Heywood to explain who he was.

"Mr. Romney!" the old man said at length. "I never expected to see you, Sir!"

"Well, here I am, Johnson!" Lord Heywood said. "I learnt from Mr. Crosswaith that you and your wife are looking after the house."

"Things aren't what they used to be, Mr. Romney, and that's a fact!" Johnson said dolefully.

Lord Heywood thought the same as he walked round to find the furniture in the rooms shrouded in Holland dust-sheets just as it had been in the country.

The house also seemed dark and smelt stuffy and dusty, but that was inevitable.

What interested him were items of furniture which Mr. Crosswaith had said were not covered by the Trust.

He found them in his mother's rooms, as he had expected, and he knew that each one was part of his childhood memories. It seemed sacrilege to sell them but there was no possible alternative.

He then looked round that part of the house which was less important, hoping that by some lucky chance he would see a painting or a piece of furniture that had escaped the eyes of his grandfather.

He found two pieces which he thought might fetch a little money, and there were also in the passages three or four paintings that might, if they were cleaned, prove to be if not valuable at least saleable.

He was aware that ever since the Regent had shown such an interest in Art it had become fashionable to appreciate paintings that in the past had been dismissed as uninteresting.

Lord Heywood had taken the trouble when he was in Paris to visit the Palaces and Museums where Napoleon had stored the treasures he had stolen from the countries he had conquered.

It made him appreciate more than he did already the old Italian and Dutch Masters.

He hoped now that there might be in the house some paintings that had not been considered interesting when his grandfather had entailed everything onto the future generations, but which in the meantime had come into fashion.

What he saw made him decide that he would get an expert to examine what was there, instead of relying entirely on the gloomy findings of Crosswaith and his Partners.

As it would obviously have been useless to ask old Johnson to provide him with any sort of luncheon, Lord Heywood decided he would go to his Club. It was growing late and it was a long time since he had breakfasted.

A hackney-carriage took him to White's in St. James's

Street, and the moment he walked in through the door he was hailed by a number of friends who were both surprised and delighted to see him after being away for so long.

Not only were they eager for him to drink with them but he had several invitations for luncheon, and he thought that at least he was not dissipating his own limited resources.

In fact, he enjoyed himself so much that it was with difficulty that he tore himself away from the Club and, having agreed to dine with three old friends, went off to the Bank.

He was in such high spirits that by the time he was shown into the Bank Manager's Office he had begun to feel as if his luck was changing and everything would be smooth sailing.

But the truth was unpalatable.

When his father had died there was a large overdraft, which had been slightly reduced by the rents from the Estate the first year after his death.

In the last two years, however, this income had ceased completely, owing to the bad economic conditions in the country, while the dividends paid by the Stocks and Shares that he owned also were very much reduced.

In fact, owing to the economic conditions, gradually the Shares themselves had become almost worthless.

"You might find a buyer for them," the Bank Manager said, "but I think, My Lord, it would be in your best interests to hold them for a year or so at least, to see if things improve."

He saw the expression on Lord Heywood's face and said quickly:

"We are promised that prosperity is round the corner, now that the Quadruple Alliance has put Europe back on its feet. So I am expecting things will soon be better in this country."

"I only hope you are right," Lord Heywood said drily, "but for the moment that does not help me personally."

When he left the Bank an hour later he had found that his position was no better than it had been before he had left the Abbey.

Actually, because now he knew the whole amount of his debts, he was more depressed than he had been before.

A visit to the Solicitors did nothing to reassure him.

Mr. Crosswaith was very sympathetic, but although under a great deal of pressure from Lord Heywood he agreed to pay the pensioners for one more month, he made it absolutely clear that he and his Partners, now that His Lordship had returned, could carry the burden of the Heywood properties no longer.

There was nothing Lord Heywood could do but thank them for their services and go from the Offices to Christie's.

These Auctioneers were recognised as having the most important and most reliable Sales-Room in London.

Lord Heywood remembered they had handled the sell-up for poor George Brummell when he had been obliged to leave the country and had also disposed of Lord Byron's effects when he had left England.

A Partner to whom he spoke understood exactly what he wanted.

"I will send one of my most reliable Valuers, My Lord, to Heywood House," he said. "I assure you if there is anything of value he will not miss it."

"I should be grateful if he would also come to the country," Lord Heywood said. "The position there is the same, and my grandfather entailed everything possible before he died. But there have been some additions, and I am hoping that perhaps in the passing years there may be a painting that has now become valuable although it was omitted from the Trust."

"That might easily have happened," Lord Heywood was told, and at least it was more encouraging than anything he had heard before.

By the time he left Christie's it was growing late and he went back to Heywood House to change into his evening-clothes which Carter had packed and put in a valise in the Curricle.

As he dressed in the bedroom which had always been occupied by his father, Lord Heywood found himself thinking of the way money had been spent over the years as if it came from an inexhaustible cornucopia.

Of course there were no horses now in the stables in the Mews where he had left Conqueror and the horse he had borrowed, but he had noted a great number of vehicles there.

Just as in the country, there were Phaetons and Curricles, Travelling-Carriages and Chariots, all out of proportion for the needs of one man.

Besides this, he was aware that since he had been abroad his father had decorated a number of rooms in a most extravagant fashion.

Heavy silk brocades on the walls of the Drawing-Room matched the elaborate curtains. In the Dining-Room the plaster-work was picked out in gold leaf, and the new painted ceiling by an Italian artist was extremely spectacular.

His father had always demanded the best, but unfortunately he did not have to pay for it.

Because he suddenly felt overwhelmed by the burden of it all, Lord Heywood wished he could run away and disappear as Lalita had done.

Then as he thought of her he found himself thinking that she would laugh at him for letting what he had learnt today get him down.

"There must be something you can do!" she would say.

There would be a note in her voice which would make him want to believe her hope that, however much he might reason to the contrary, even at the last moment a miracle would save him.

"She has certainly kept me more cheerful than I might otherwise have been," he admitted, and decided that the sooner he got back to the country the better.

Feeling smart in his evening-clothes although they were tight under the arms and across the shoulders, Lord Heywood walked down the staircase.

Old Johnson was waiting in the Hall.

"I ought to 'ave told Your Lordship that th' Carrier from Dover brought some luggage 'ere yesterday, but it went straight out o' me mind."

"I was going to ask you about that," Lord Heywood replied. "I had everything I brought back from France sent here, and now that it has arrived I will take it back with me tomorrow."

He had to repeat this several times before Johnson got it into his head. Then the Butler said:

"And there's some letters too, M'Lord. They've been arriving almost every day for Your Lordship."

One glance at the letters which reposed on a silver salver told Lord Heywood whom they were from.

There was no mistaking Irene Dawlish's flowery and elaborate handwriting, and he thought with a sinking of his heart that she must be back in England.

This made him say hastily:

"I will look at them when I get back, Johnson. Please

ask your wife if she will give me breakfast at eight o'clock tomorrow morning. I wish to leave early."

"What hour did you say, M'Lord?"

"Eight o'clock," Lord Heywood repeated.

Then, ignoring the letters, he hurried out of the house to his Club.

Once again he enjoyed himself until a little later in the evening one of his friends said:

"Somebody was asking after you, Heywood, and when I told her you were in London she was extremely interested."

"Who was that?" Lord Heywood managed to ask with a very convincing air of indifference.

"Irene Dawlish! I gather you saw a great deal of her when you were both in Paris."

There was a note of undoubted jealousy in his informant's voice and Lord Heywood replied:

"I can assure you I was not the only one. Lady Irene was a huge success with, I might say, almost the whole Army of Occupation!"

There was laughter at this and another man remarked:

"The Army would just about satisfy the beautiful Irene! We should send her as an emissary to the next Conference. She would undoubtedly invigorate the delegates and prove a very able Ambassador!"

"Why do you not make the suggestion to the Foreign Secretary and perhaps it should come before Parliament!" somebody joked.

"Personally, I am against the export of beautiful women," another man quipped.

Later, thinking over what had been said Lord Heywood told himself it was the sort of discussion he would not like to hear about his wife, if he had one.

When he went up to bed he opened two of the letters from Lady Irene and found, as he had expected, that she was not only very insistent on seeing him but was also extremely possessive.

He was forced to accept the awkward fact that she intended to marry him, and their having been apart appeared to have made her more determined and certainly more ardent in her pursuit of him than she had been before.

Her letters were passionate and flattering. At the same time, Lord Heywood wondered how many times before she had used the same flowery phrases and the same inciting words to a man with whom she thought herself to be in love.

'I am only one of many men she has tried to tie to herself,' he thought.

At the same time, he was not so foolish as not to be aware that what should have been a light and enjoyable *affair de coeur* had got out of hand.

Most of the women he had made love to had remained friends with him when their affair was over.

But their feelings were inevitably more deeply involved than his, and although he was uncomfortably aware that one or two of them had believed their hearts were broken, he had not tried to avoid them or to forget the happiness they had found together.

With Lady Irene it was different.

He was sure she was aware that as far as he was concerned their liaison, for that was what it had been, had come to an end, but she was determined not to let him go.

He thought, as he had before, that never in his wildest dreams had he imagined that she would wish to marry him.

She had made no secret of the fact that she had had a large number of lovers in her life, and if he had considered it at all, which he had not, he would have thought that if she remarried it would have been to somebody of more importance than himself.

That she had appreciated him as a lover was not unusual. But that she should be satisfied with marrying a mere Baron even though he had a magnificent house was somehow out-of-character.

It was then, as he thought of it, that Lord Heywood had the uncomfortable thought that perhaps for the first time in her life Lady Irene was really in love.

Not love as he thought of it, and which he never expected to find, but a love that was almost entirely physical and as such was violent, with something primitive and animal-like about it.

All of a sudden he was aware that Lady Irene would fight like a tiger to capture and hold her prey, which was himself.

He hoped he was exaggerating the whole situation and being absurdly imaginative.

Then as he undressed he saw that the note lying on the top of the chest-of-drawers was open and the words and phrases seemed to leap out at him as if they were written in letters of fire.

After such a long day he had expected he would fall asleep as soon as he touched the pillow, but he found himself instead lying awake, thinking of Irene and wondering how he could escape from her.

He had hoped when he left Paris that she would forget about him.

At the Balls which were given every night she had undoubtedly shone like a star and easily eclipsed the other beauties whether they were French or English.

There were numbers of men ready to squire her and several who, to Lord Heywood's knowledge, had fancied themselves in love with her.

Yet when she clung to him the night before he left she had said:

"We belong to each other, Romney, and this is true, I want you and I know that I cannot live without you."

"You certainly cannot live with me!" Lord Heywood had replied lightly. "I am going back to a house without servants, an Estate that is heavily in debt, and a future that is so problematical that I am afraid of it myself!"

"What does any of that matter except that I love you?" Lady Irene asked. "I have enough money for us both at the moment, and because Richard is dead Papa will leave everything to me."

The way she had spoken about her brother, who had been killed in action two years earlier, shocked Lord Heywood.

He remembered that the Marquis of Mortlike had been broken-hearted at losing his only son.

Before he had met Lady Irene he had always been sorry for her for having lost both her brother and her husband, only to learn that Dawlish's death had hardly affected her and now she could speak casually of her nearest relative.

He had unfastened her arms from round his neck and said:

"If you are proposing to me, Irene, although I am deeply honoured, my answer is quite simply 'No'!"

Lady Irene gave a cry of protest and flung herself against him.

"Do you really believe I would allow you to refuse me? I love you, Romney, I love you! I love you! And nothing and nobody in the world shall take you from me!"

Lord Heywood had been unable to reply, for she was kissing him with burning lips and his protests were swept away by a fire that seemed to consume her with a violence that he had never known in any other woman.

"More damned trouble!" he said to himself now in the darkness.

Then he found himself thinking of how he would tell Lalita all about his visits to the Bank, the Solicitors, and Christie's.

'She will understand,' he thought.

He did not ask himself why he was so sure that she would do so.

*　　*　　*

On the drive home, the horses, having rested, were as spirited as they had been the previous day, and Lord Heywood had the feeling that he was escaping from Lady Irene.

He had risen early, but Mrs. Johnson, who was very slow in her movements, had kept him waiting for breakfast, and just before he was ready to go to the Mews to harness the horses to the Curricle, a note was delivered by a groom wearing a livery that Lord Heywood recognised.

He was in the Hall when Johnson opened the door and he heard the groom say:

"Here's another love-token, an' if I goes on playin' Cupid, I'll be growin' wings!"

The groom had not waited for Johnson to reply but had remounted his horse and trotted away.

The old Butler had looked round for the salver in which to place the note before handing it to his Master.

"Put it on the table," Lord Heywood had said, "and if anybody enquires, inform them that I had left before I could receive it."

It took some minutes to make Johnson understand, and when he did the old man said:

"If 'er Ladyship asks, shall I tell 'er where Your Lordship's gone?"

"Unfortunately, she will be able to deduce that for herself," Lord Heywood replied.

Because this made him even more determined than ever to leave London, Lord Heywood had gone to the kitchen to thank Mrs. Johnson for the breakfast, had given old Johnson a guinea, which had delighted him, then had left the house by the back-door which led into the Mews.

"If I evade Irene for long enough," he told himself when he was free of the London traffic, "I am sure she will tire of the pursuit and find somebody else on whom she can concentrate."

It was a pleasant idea. At the same time, he had the uncomfortable feeling that she would not be so easily distracted from her objective.

Now that he thought about it seriously, he realised there were not so many unattached men of the right age to offer her marriage.

He knew that young girls belonging to the aristocracy were pushed up the aisle by their parents as early as possible. And the same applied to their sons as soon as they came of age.

How they behaved afterwards was entirely their own business, but it was expected of a man that he should enjoy himself, and those who constituted the Carlton House Set followed the example of the Regent by being invariably engaged in a love-affair with some delectable beauty or other.

To have reached the age of thirty-two without being encumbered with a wife was, Lord Heywood realised, almost unique.

When he considered the men who pursued Lady

Irene ardently, there was hardly one, except himself, who was in a position to offer her marriage.

There were several whom he considered "beardless boys" who were younger than she was, and if she accepted their advances on a permanent basis it would make her a laughing-stock.

"I have never thought of it before," he told himself with a wry smile, "but, impoverished though I may be, I still have a certain value in the marriage-market!"

He had always despised the way mothers, ambitious for their daughters, married them to dissolute Peers almost before they had left the School-Room, so that they could be what was called "settled in life," and the more impressive the title, the more brilliant the marriage.

It was never a case of their hearts being involved or love being part of the contract.

"Love is something which comes after marriage and not before," he had heard one cynic say, and he knew that was true as far as the *Beau Monde* was concerned.

"When I marry, and it is very problematical whether I shall ever do so," Lord Heywood told himself, "it will be because I love the woman who is my wife and with whom I am content to spend the rest of my life."

He knew now that the one thing he would never tolerate was a wife who was unfaithful to him, any more than he would wish to be unfaithful to her.

He knew that almost any man of his acquaintance, especially those with whom he had laughed and talked last night, would consider him a fool to have such ideas.

And yet, although he had never spoken of these ideas to anybody, they were there, and because of it he would never marry except for love, however advantageous it might be from a worldly point of view.

He had known perceptively, although Mr. Crosswaith was far too tactful to put it into words, what was at the back of the Solicitor's mind as they had talked over his difficulties.

Lord Heywood could read his thoughts, and knew he was thinking as they sat opposite each other that as a presentable young man with a title and a house that was the envy of everybody who had ever seen it, it would be very easy for him to find a rich wife.

She would gladly pay off his debts and provide him with the comfort which he deserved after the long years of war.

It seemed to Lord Heywood that Mr. Crosswaith had almost said this aloud, and with difficulty he had prevented himself from replying sharply that he had no intention of living on his wife's money and adding that if there was no other way of saving the Abbey, it would just have to tumble down on his head.

Then Mr. Crosswaith had spoken of other things and Lord Heywood forgot what he had been thinking.

Now it was back in his mind, and as he reached the open road where he could give the horses their heads, he thought that he was gradually moving away from the menace which had seemed real to him while he was in London.

At the same time, he was well aware that he had not yet escaped.

He might have left Lady Irene's letters unopened, but she knew he had come to London and gone away again without seeing her, and he could almost hear her voice saying passionately, fiercely:

"We belong to each other, Romney, and I will never let you go!"

Chapter Five

As he drove down the drive Lord Heywood thought the Abbey was looking unusually beautiful despite the fact that the sky was overcast.

It had been a hot day with little air, and he had felt cooler when driving his horses very fast than if he had been forced to go more slowly.

Now because he was home he felt as if the sun had come out, and although he knew it was regrettably far from reality, the Abbey seemed to stand for security and safety.

Over the last miles, as if they knew their own stables were just ahead of them, Conqueror and his companion had moved faster without any encouragement from their driver.

Now they swept in style round the gravel courtyard to come to a standstill at the bottom of the steps.

As they did so Carter came hurrying down them, and as he ran to the horses' heads he said:

"Welcome back, M'Lord!"

Lord Heywood put down the reins to step from the

Curricle, thinking as he did so that it was strange there was no sign of Lalita.

With a feeling that struck him quite unawares, he had a sudden fear that, just as she had arrived unannounced at the Abbey, she had left in the same way.

He would have asked Carter where she was, but he was already walking the horses towards the stables.

Then as Lord Heywood started to climb the steps there was a cry from the top of them and Lalita came dashing down towards him almost as if she were carried on wings.

She met him halfway, and with an exclamation of joy that seemed to lilt on the air she flung her arms round him, hugging him as a child might have done, and kissed his cheek.

"You are back!" she cried. "I was so afraid you would be delayed and we would wait for you in vain."

She took her arms from round him to walk beside him into the Hall, slipping her hand in his as she did so.

"What happened?" she asked. "I must know."

There was something so young and eager in the way she spoke that as Lord Heywood with his free hand put his hat down on the table, he felt that even though he had nothing very new or encouraging to relate, it was somehow good news.

"Come and tell me all about it," Lalita said before he could speak. "I have everything ready for you in the Writing-Room."

Still holding his hand, she pulled him towards it and as he entered the room Lord Heywood saw there were vases of flowers on the tables and desk, a bottle of wine in an ice-bucket, and a large pitcher he had not seen before.

Lalita released his hand and went to the table.

"You must be thirsty," she said. "It has been very hot today and I am sure the roads were dusty."

The way she spoke told Lord Heywood that she had something with which to quench his thirst, and he smiled as he replied:

"You are quite right. I am thirsty!"

"I was sure you would be," Lalita said. "Carter was sure you would prefer wine, but I have my peach-juice ready for you."

She looked at him anxiously as she spoke, and he answered:

"I can imagine nothing I would enjoy more!"

She gave an exclamation of pleasure and came towards him with a cut-glass tumbler in one hand and the pitcher in the other.

As he settled himself in a comfortable chair and watched her pour the peach-juice into the tumbler, Lord Heywood thought he might be a married man returning home to a very attentive wife.

He raised the glass to his lips and knew that Lalita was awaiting his verdict.

"It is delicious!" he declared. "Really delicious! I have never tasted anything like it!"

"I knew you would be pleased," she said with a smile.

She waited until he had drunk some more of the juice, then topped up the glass before she took the pitcher back to the table.

Then she ran back to him to sit not in a chair at his side but on the rug at his feet.

She looked very young and very lovely as she raised her eyes to his to ask anxiously:

"Were you successful?"

"In obtaining a loan? No!"

Her smile faded.

"I prayed so very hard, and I was sure my prayers would be answered."

"Well, they may be, in a less direct way," Lord Heywood said. "I found some furniture and paintings at Heywood House, which I hope will bring in some money, and a Valuer will be looking at them this week."

"That is good!"

"He will also be coming here, and I have persuaded the Solicitors to pay the pensioners for this month, so it gives us a little breathing-space."

"You have been clever, very clever, I can see that!"

"Not as clever as I would like to be," Lord Heywood answered, "but you continue your prayers and hope that the Valuer will find something worthwhile."

"I shall do that, you know I will!"

Lalita then told him how busy she and Carter had been in the greenhouses.

"We picked all the peaches that were ripe," she said, "and Carter found some jars in which he could bottle them. In that way we can eat them when there is no longer any fruit in the garden."

The way she spoke told Lord Heywood that she was thinking of the winter. He told himself that she would certainly not be here with him then, but it would be unkind to say so.

She chatted away, telling him things that were trivial but to him were interesting, and he found himself just as much amused as he had been the day before by the gossip he had listened to in the Club.

"Now tell me where you had luncheon and where you dined," Lalita said.

She listened attentively as he described not only his friends but the food he had eaten and some of the conversations which had taken place.

"It all sounds very exciting!" she said when he had finished. "But did you not have time to go dancing or visit some of your other . . . friends in their houses?"

He knew by the way she hesitated over the words that what she wanted to say was "lady-friends."

"I had a very pleasant evening," he replied, "and when I left the Club I was ready to go to bed."

He thought he saw an expression of relief on Lalita's face, then he told himself that he should not have to be accountable for his actions to a child who was staying with him as an uninvited guest.

"I hope you did not have a very big luncheon," she said, breaking in on his thoughts.

"As a matter of fact I stopped in a small village. The horse I borrowed from the farm cast a shoe and while it was being shod I ate bread and cheese and drank a pewter of beer with the old cronies sitting outside."

"They must have enjoyed that," Lalita said. "But Carter and I have a really gastronomic dinner for you tonight, so I want you to be hungry."

"I shall be," Lord Heywood answered.

He saw Lalita's eyes light up, and almost as if even the weather brightened because he was home, the sun came out from behind the clouds and shone through the open windows to turn her hair to gold.

She looked so pretty sitting at his feet that he thought she resembled the flowers that she had arranged in the vases, giving the room a beauty which he knew had been missing before.

Then as Lalita looked up at him as if she wondered what he was thinking, their eyes met and for a moment it was difficult for Lord Heywood to look away.

* * *

Introducing the Romantic World of Barbara Cartland Fragrances

A world of rare and exotic perfumes…
Inspired by the intensely romantic raptures
of love in every Barbara Cartland novel.

Experience the World of Barbara Cartland Fragrances

Awaken the romantic in your soul. With the mysteriously beautiful perfumes of romance inspired by Barbara Cartland. There's a heady floral bouquet called *The Heart Triumphant,* an exotic Oriental essence named *Moments of Love* and *Love Wins,* a tantalizing woodsy floral. Each of the three, blended with the poetry and promise of love. For every woman who has ever yearned to love. Yesterday, today and especially tomorrow!

Available at fragrance counters everywhere.

Helena Rubinstein®

Introducing the Romantic World of Barbara Cartland Fragrances

A world of rare and exotic perfumes…
Inspired by the intensely romantic raptures
of love in every Barbara Cartland novel.

There was plenty to do before he went upstairs to change.

In his bedroom he found that Carter had prepared a bath for him, and afterwards when he had dressed himself in the evening-clothes which had belonged to his father and which were larger and therefore slightly more comfortable than his own, he found himself looking forward to dinner with an eagerness which made him laugh at himself.

'I should be depressed and worried by the failure of my mission,' he thought.

Instead, he found himself appreciating the Abbey in a different way from what he had felt when he had first returned.

He might not be allowed to sell the paintings and the furniture but they were his for his lifetime.

There might not be footmen in the Hall and house-maids to sweep away the dust that was still accumulating behind the closed doors, but he had Carter and Lalita, and for the moment he was content not to ask for anything more.

When he entered the Dining-Room he realised how hard the two of them had worked to make a celebration dinner for his return.

Tonight he was to eat at the big table instead of the little one in the window, and in front of his high-backed chair which bore his coat-of-arms there was a large silver candelabrum holding six candles.

There were also laid out on the table various silver ornaments which he had forgotten he possessed.

They were shining brilliantly in the candlelight and Lord Heywood knew that Carter and Lalita must have expended a great deal of time in cleaning them.

Lalita had just started lighting the candles in the Dining-Room when he had come downstairs, and he saw with a smile that she was wearing an evening-gown that he had not seen before, and round her neck was a diamond necklace.

There was also a diamond brooch in her hair and a bracelet of the same gems round her wrist.

As he walked towards her she curtseyed, and there was a look of almost childish excitement on her face as if she were at a party.

"You are certainly celebrating my home-coming in style!" Lord Heywood said. "Thank you, Lalita!"

"This is how Your Lordship should always be served," she said, "and tonight there must be no problems, no difficulties about the future, and you must just enjoy yourself."

"That is what I intend to do," he replied.

He sat down and found there was a glass of madeira already poured out for him.

As he sipped it he said:

"I must drink your health, Lalita, and later I will thank you for what I can sense already is going to be a very special evening."

Carter, dressed in the Heywood livery with its crested silver buttons, came in with the first course, and Lord Heywood guessed that it must have been Lalita who was aware exactly what wine should go with each dish and had searched the cellar for them.

When finally a bottle of champagne appeared with the Peach Sorbet which Carter had made exceptionally well, Lord Heywood said:

"I suppose you know you have given me another clue. Your father must have enjoyed both good food and good wine for you to be so knowledgeable about it."

"That is true, but my grandfather taught me more than anybody else did."

"I will make a note of it in my dossier about you."

"I have a feeling it does not yet consist of many pages!"

"You would be surprised what I do know!" Lord Heywood replied, knowing it would make her curious.

"A dossier should contain not only facts about my life but your estimation of my character," she remarked.

"Of course," he agreed.

"I have often wondered what you do . . . think of me."

Lord Heywood laughed.

"This is the first time I have known you to be really feminine. All women are curious to know how others think of them, but you appeared to be the exception."

"I am only curious about what you think," Lalita answered, "and if you would like to give me an estimation of my character, I will reply with yours."

Lord Heywood sat back comfortably in his chair, a glass of champagne in his hand.

"Ladies first!" he said. "I should be interested to know what you think of me."

Lalita put her head a little on one side, which was, as he had thought before, a very attractive gesture and made him think of a small bird.

"Now, let me think," she said slowly. "You know of course that you are strong, determined, domineering, and overwhelming! A lot of people must have told you that."

Lord Heywood raised his eye-brows but he did not say anything.

"But you are also," Lalita said, "kind, compassionate, understanding, and intuitive."

"How can you know that?" he enquired.

"I can feel it when you send out vibrations from yourself towards another person like me. It is almost as if you are sending what I am feeling and thinking and in fact delving beneath the surface."

She spoke slowly and carefully, then made a sudden little gesture with her hands as she said:

"I am explaining myself badly, so you must use your intuition to understand what I am trying to say."

"I do understand," Lord Heywood said, "and I find it surprising."

"Why?"

"Because I think it is something that nobody has ever discovered about me before."

She smiled and it brought the mischief back into her eyes.

"I told you I was a Celt, and although you will not believe me, I know that everything in the future is going to be . . . exactly as you . . . wish it to be."

"I would like to believe that."

"You can believe it because it is true," Lalita insisted. "You will win because you always win, because you are a victor, a conqueror, a man who will vanquish his enemies, whether they are people or situations."

Lord Heywood raised his glass.

"Tonight, after such a good dinner in such charming company," he said, "I am prepared to believe in anything, even in the crock of gold at the foot of the rainbow."

"That is what you will find," Lalita said in a soft voice.

There was silence until she asked:

"Now tell me what you think of me."

"Determined, obstinate, contradictory, disobedient," he teased.

Lalita gave a cry of protest and he added:

"But imaginative, understanding, gentle, and very lovely."

For the first time since he had known her, Lalita looked shy and blushed.

Having congratulated Carter on the dinner, they went back into the Writing-Room where Lalita showed Lord Heywood an old book she had found on the shelves when she was dusting.

It described the Abbey as it had been originally and contained a plan showing what parts of the old building had been preserved when it was rebuilt by Robert Adam.

"One of the Chapels is just as it was when the Monks were here," Lalita said. "As soon as I have time I am going to clean it out, put flowers and candles on the altar, and pray that those who first lived in the Abbey will come back to bless us."

"I am glad you think that can happen," Lord Heywood said.

As she showed him the pictures he was conscious of how close she was to him as they sat side by side on the sofa, but she was concentrating on turning over the pages.

He was aware that she smelt of roses and he could feel the warmth of her body against his side.

Because she was wearing an evening-gown there was something very soft and feminine about her, and he found it difficult not to put his arms round her and draw her closer.

It struck him that it was unprecedented for any woman to be sitting as near to him as Lalita was without raising her lips invitingly to his and attempting to excite him physically.

Lady Irene's face seemed to flash before his eyes, and once again he was thankful that he had left her behind in London.

"I wish Robert Adam had left a great deal more of the

old Abbey," Lalita was saying. "It must have been not only beautiful but sanctified."

"We still have the Chapel," Lord Heywood said, "and you are right, Lalita, we must clean it up and make it as it was when I was a boy, a place of quietness and prayer."

"If we can do that I shall pray there for you every day!" Lalita promised.

She shut the book and walked across the room to put it back in its place.

Lord Heywood watched her, thinking she had a grace that was as natural as her lack of self-consciousness.

He also thought that in her elegant evening-gown with diamonds at her throat she would be the Belle at any Ball she attended, and she was certainly wasting her youth and beauty on a man who had nothing to offer her but a roof over her head.

Aloud he said:

"Have you thought, Lalita, that the most effective way you could dispose of your Guardian from whom you are hiding would be to get married?"

She turned quickly from the book-shelves to face him.

"Married . . . ?"

"Your uncle would have no jurisdiction over you if you had a husband."

He saw by the expression on her face that she was thinking in horror of the imbecile to whom her uncle had tried to marry her, and he added quickly:

"There are a great number of men in the world who would, I am sure, be only too eager to offer for you, if you had the chance of meeting them."

The expression of horror faded from Lalita's face.

"Are you suggesting you might give a Ball for me?" she enquired.

"I would do that if it were possible, but I was really thinking that you should take your rightful place in Society."

"I am not sure that I have a rightful place," she said, "but if you will not give a Ball for me, the next time we have a celebration dinner we must find out if there is a fiddler in the village so that we can invite him here and I can dance with you."

Before Lord Heywood could speak she clapped her hands.

"That is a wonderful idea! And of course if we blindfold him he would not be able to see me, although he might think it rather strange if you were dancing alone with yourself."

Lord Heywood laughed.

"You are making it into a fairy-story, Lalita, but I was being serious in thinking that it is a mistake to waste your youth and beauty on an old man like me."

"Now you are definitely fishing for compliments!" Lalita said. "I think what I am really doing is monopolising you and keeping away all those busy little bees who hover round a honey-pot which is called 'Romney Heywood'!"

"You have been talking to Carter!" Lord Heywood said accusingly.

"Of course I have. He has made me realise how very privileged I am to dine alone with a man who must have broken hundreds of hearts in his time."

"If you talk to me like that I shall be extremely angry!"

Lord Heywood tried to speak severely, but his eyes were twinkling.

Lalita crossed the room to sit down again at his feet, her gown billowing out round her so that she looked more than ever like a rose just coming into bloom.

"I will not tease you," she said, "because my instinct tells me you are very sensitive . . . about your attractions. Instead, I will just say I would rather be here dining with you than dancing at Almack's or attending a Ball at Devonshire House."

"I still say that is where you should be."

"And my reply is the same: I am very . . . very . . . happy where I . . . am."

There was no doubt of the sincerity in her voice, which shone in her eyes, making her look so lovely that Lord Heywood had to check an almost irresistible impulse to draw her closer to him again and kiss her lips.

*   *   *

The next morning they went riding early as usual, and Lord Heywood felt again as if everything he looked at, everything he saw, meant more to him than it had before he had left for London.

He did not say anything to Lalita, but as if she was aware of it she said as they settled down to a trot:

"Nothing is worth having unless one has to fight for it."

"Why do you say that?"

"Because I was thinking last night that most people are so taken up with the little difficulties and frustrations in life that they are inclined to take the big things for granted."

Lord Heywood was well aware of what she was saying, and he answered:

"Money is to most people a big thing."

"Only when they have none," Lalita replied with unassailable logic.

She glanced at him from under her eye-lashes as she said:

"My mother used to say to me when I was a child:

'Count your blessings,' and I think if you start off with
the Abbey and end up with Waterloo, you have not
done badly."

"You are preaching at me," Lord Heywood protested, "and I consider it a vast impertinence on your
part."

"I think really I am envying you," Lalita answered.
"Poor or rich, big or small, what everybody wants is a
home, and that is something I have lost and may never
have again."

There was something very wistful in the way she
spoke, and Lord Heywood said without thinking:

"I thought for the moment you were sharing mine."

"That is what I pretend I am doing," Lalita said, "but
at the same time, as you well know, I am always afraid
that you may turn me out."

"I am still trying to think what is the best for you."

"I can give you the answer to that quite easily,"
Lalita said, "but before we get serious, I suggest I race
you to those trees, and it is only fair that I should have
a good start."

As she spoke she touched Conqueror with her whip
and was away at so swift a gallop that it took Lord
Heywood some minutes before he could catch up with
her.

As soon as they arrived back at the Abbey they
started to clean the Chapel, and it was obvious that it
had been neglected perhaps more than any other room
in the house.

It was not only that the dust had accumulated, but
some of the panes of glass in the windows were broken
and the birds had come in to nest on the elaborate
cornice and even on the triptych above the altar.

However, the carvings round the wall were as fine as
when they had been placed there by the Monks, and

the marble of the altar itself when washed had a beauty which only age could impart.

They worked until luncheon-time, then after they had cleaned themselves up and eaten the excellent rabbit-stew which Carter had prepared for them, Lord Heywood said:

"I think we have done enough in the Chapel for today. I suggest we rest for a little while, while it is still rather hot, then go into the garden."

"I would like that," Lalita answered.

"I want to show you where my mother once planted a water-garden," Lord Heywood went on. "I am afraid now it will be overgrown and full of weeds, but it used to have little waterfalls and pools in which there were goldfish. Perhaps one day we shall be able to restore it to the way it looked when I was a boy."

He had spoken without thinking, and only as he saw Lalita looking up at him was he aware that he had implied that she would be with him for a long time.

'I must not raise her hopes,' he thought to himself severely.

"That would be fun," Lalita agreed, "and I have something else to show to you, if you have time."

"What is that?"

"Some drawings that I discovered in a drawer in what I believe is known as the Heraldry-Room. They are very interesting and they might be valuable if they were executed by an artist of any note."

"I would like to see them," Lord Heywood replied.

"They are so pretty that I am sure you will hate to part with them," Lalita said. "I think really they should be framed and hung on the walls."

"I know very little about drawings," Lord Heywood admitted, "but this is something we will ask about when the man from Christie's visits here."

He refused a glass of port that Carter offered him, saying:

"I shall be getting fat, Carter, if you feed me so well, and that reminds me—you must be getting short of money. In fact, I suspect you are in debt, which is something I cannot allow."

Lord Heywood was quite unconscious of the glance that passed between Carter and Lalita.

"As it 'appens, M'Lord," Carter said, "I was waiting for Your Lordship's return so that I could ask for a guinea or two."

Lord Heywood put his hand in his pocket.

"Actually I have that with me now," he said, "and mind you pay the proper price for everything we buy."

"We do that, M'Lord."

"Don't forget," Lord Heywood insisted.

As he spoke, Carter walked out through the doorway and Lalita gave a sigh of relief.

Lord Heywood obviously had no idea how much she and Carter had spent already on the food he found so delicious.

Because she had no wish to dwell on the subject, she talked to him animatedly of the drawings she had to show him, and when they reached the Writing-Room she sat down in her favourite position at his feet to take the sketches from a portfolio and spread them out round her.

"Look at this one!" she said. "It is exquisite!"

"I think it must be of Rome," Lord Heywood said, "and it is certainly drawn by a very accomplished artist."

"That is what I thought, and although I have never been there I am sure this is a view of Paris."

"It is indeed!" Lord Heywood agreed. "In fact, I remember standing in that actual place!"

"With whom?" Lalita asked.

"I can hear the suspicion in your voice," he replied. "But actually I was with a crusty old General who had imbibed too much at luncheon and I was having some difficulty in keeping him on his feet."

"How unromantic!"

Lalita threw back her head and laughed.

As she did so the door opened and the sound died on her lips.

Coming into the room and looking like a vision from another world was the most beautiful woman she had ever seen.

Dressed in a silk pelisse of shimmering green and a pointed bonnet trimmed with ostrich-feathers of the same colour, she was so sensational that it flashed through Lalita's mind that she must be an actress.

Then as Lord Heywood rose to his feet she heard him exclaim almost beneath his breath:

"Irene!"

So this, Lalita thought, was the famous Lady Irene of whom Carter had spoken and whom Lord Heywood had been glad to leave behind in Paris!

As she swept into the room there was a smile on her red lips and a glint in her eyes behind her heavily mascaraed eye-lashes.

Then as she looked first at Lord Heywood and then at Lalita, the smile vanished.

"How could you come to London, Romney, without seeing me?" she asked sharply.

Then looking at Lalita she demanded:

"Who is this? And what is she doing here?"

There was no mistaking the anger behind the last words, and as Lalita rose to her feet and Lady Irene came farther into the room, she could see suspicion and antagonism in the look on her face.

Lalita was aware in that second that she had to save Lord Heywood from this woman.

She was thinking not of herself but of him, for she knew that Lady Irene, having found them alone at the Abbey, could raise a scandal that would do him irreparable damage.

Acting on an impulse which seemed to come to her as if it were an inspiration from above, she walked towards Lady Irene, holding out her hand.

"I think," she said with a smile, "that you must be Lady Irene Dawlish. I have been looking forward to meeting you because I have heard so much about you from my . . . husband."

As Lalita finished speaking she thought that the two other people in the room seemed to have been turned to stone.

Then in a voice that sounded strangled Lady Irene asked:

"Did you say—your husband?"

Lalita did not dare look at Lord Heywood but kept her eyes on the face of the woman in front of her.

"Yes . . . we are . . . married," she said, "but it has to be a . . . secret because I am in . . . mourning for my grandfather. But I know you will understand and say nothing about it until we can announce it properly."

"Married!" Lady Irene exclaimed, and now the words seemed to echo round the room.

She took a step forward to face Lord Heywood.

"How can you have done this to me?" she asked. "You have ignored all my letters, you have made no effort to get in touch with me, and now I learn you are—married!"

Her voice rose as she went on:

"I have never been so insulted and I consider your behaviour abominable!"

With an obvious effort Lord Heywood found his voice.

"If I have upset you, I can only apologise."

"Upset me?" Lady Irene repeated. "How did you expect me to feel? When you left me you said . . ."

She threw up her hands.

"But what is the point of talking about it? You are married, and I believed—I hoped—!"

Words failed her.

Then as if she suddenly lost all control of herself she stamped her foot.

"You will be sorry you have done this to me!" she threatened. "And I will make sure that this milk-faced chit is not accepted by any decent people!"

She almost shouted the last word, then turned and swept from the room in a flurry of silk that seemed to rustle round her like the hiss of a snake.

They listened to her footsteps going down the passage, until as if Lord Heywood somewhat belatedly remembered his good manners he hurried after her.

Only when she was alone did Lalita feel as if her legs would no longer carry her, and she sank down again on the floor.

Then she asked herself what she had done.

It had all happened so quickly, and the explanation that they were married had come to her lips without her even for a second considering the implications of it.

And yet, if Carter was right—as indeed her coming here had confirmed—Lady Irene's pursuit of Lord Heywood was not something he wanted, and if she was trying to marry him she would now realise that it was a hopeless idea and would leave him alone.

Then Lalita was afraid it would not be as easy as that, and when she heard Lord Heywood's footsteps coming slowly back down the passage she realised that she was trembling.

Because she could not bear to look at his face to see what he was feeling, she started to pick up the sketches that were spread out on the floor and heard him shut the door behind him.

He came towards her to stand a few feet away, and she knew he was waiting for her to look up at him.

"I suppose you realise what you have done!" he said, and she thought his voice was severe and accusing.

"I thought . . . I was helping . . . you."

"And having done so you have got yourself into more of a mess than you were in already!"

"I . . . I cannot see . . . why it should . . . affect me."

"Do not be so stupid!" Lord Heywood said sharply. "What is going to happen when my friends are told that we are married and wish to congratulate me?"

"You could . . . say the whole thing was a . . . joke, and that would mean the laugh was on Lady Irene."

Lord Heywood could not help thinking it was a rather ingenious explanation. At the same time, he was certain that there would be far more serious repercussions than that.

He walked to the window as if looking out into the garden would help him to think.

"If . . . I have . . . done anything to . . . harm you," Lalita said, "then I . . . I will . . . go at once."

"I do not understand why you did it."

"Carter told me . . . that you had been . . . glad to leave her . . . behind in Paris."

"Carter had no right to say such things."

"But it was . . . true?"

"I do not intend to discuss it."

"But . . . she would be . . . wrong for you . . . if you were thinking of . . . marrying her! She is not a . . . good woman."

"How can you know that?" Lord Heywood asked in an exasperated voice.

"But I do know! She is bad . . . I promise you she is! And now that she is angry she will . . . hurt you if she . . . can."

Lord Heywood was aware that this was the truth and it was impossible for him to refute it.

Yet, because he really was bemused by what had occurred, he had no wish to make explanations to Lalita, glad as he was to be rid of Irene.

It was an easy way out, yet because Lalita was irretrievably involved it infuriated him, and he walked out of the Writing-Room, slamming the door behind him.

*   *   *

Lalita sat staring blindly at the drawings and felt the tears come into her eyes.

She had wanted only to help him.

She had wanted to protect him from Lady Irene, who even before she had seen her she had thought must be bad, but now she was sure she was worse than that. She was in some way positively evil!

She thought the vibrations coming from Lady Irene were very much the same as those which had come from her uncle when he was trying to force her into marriage with her cousin Philip.

And she knew that she must save Lord Heywood from a woman who eventually would disillusion and hurt him.

As she thought about him, Lalita was sure that although he was very reserved about himself he had the high ideals that she had always imagined a good and brave man would have in his heart.

She had thought this morning when they were cleaning out the Chapel that only a man who believed in

God and was essentially noble would have been so willing to brush away the dust and dirt in that sacred place.

Using what she thought of as her Celtic instinct, she was sure that that was how he had thought of it, but now it was just another room in the Abbey.

"When he marries," she told herself, "it must be to a woman who will inspire him to do chivalrous deeds and be worthy of the Monks who built this Abbey to the glory of God."

She felt almost as if they were helping her to protect Lord Heywood, and although he might be angry with her now, perhaps later he would understand why she had acted as she had and realise that he was well rid of Lady Irene.

"I hate her!" Lalita said to herself, as she thought how happy they had been before she arrived.

The beautiful woman had brought a darkness and a sense of insecurity into the Abbey that had never been there before, and as if she had already besmirched the atmosphere of the room, Lalita went to the windows to open them wider than they were already.

As she did so she saw that like yesterday, although it was very hot, the sky was overcast.

'It looks as if it is going to rain,' she thought, 'and I hope Her Ladyship has a wet drive back to London!'

It was a childish wish and Lalita was aware of it.

She knew that what was really worrying her was that Lord Heywood was angry. How could she coax him back into happiness again?

"Please, God, go on helping me for a little while longer," she prayed.

But in her apprehension she felt as if there were a stone in her breast growing larger and heavier with every moment.

She looked up at the grey sky.

"Please . . . please," she pleaded.

But there was no sunshine to give her the answer she desired.

Chapter Six

Lord Heywood, lying on his bed, was not thinking of the heat, although it was excessive.

Before he got into bed he had pulled back the curtains and opened the windows wide. He thought that the heat, which had made it hard to breathe all day, was even worse than it had been before.

His mind, however, was preoccupied with Lalita, and actually he was feeling ashamed.

He had almost been thrown off his balance by what had occurred, and he knew now, if he was honest, that he had "taken out" his irritation on her.

When he had left her in the Writing-Room he had gone for a long walk in the woods behind the house, making himself unpleasantly hot but finding that it did little to soothe his feelings.

He felt as if a new problem, more insurmountable than ever, had arisen, and although he had been concerned over Lalita before, he now felt that the position in which she placed herself made it imperative that he should do something about her.

The question was—what could that be?

He was quite sure that when Lady Irene arrived back in London the story that he was married to somebody completely unknown would lose nothing in the telling.

She was not the type of woman to nurse in silence any hurt she received.

Instead, she would do her best to evoke sympathy from everybody she knew and would try to make them condemn him for being heartless and unfaithful.

Because quite a lot of her admirers would be only too glad to see him out of the running, they would not only agree with her but would do their best to defame him in the Clubs.

As a matter of fact, since Lady Irene was well known to be promiscuous, the more sensible men would merely laugh and think he was wise to have escaped while he could.

But the women would chatter and naturally their curiosity would be centred on the woman who had taken Lady Irene's place and vanquished her in the process.

"What shall I do about it?" Lord Heywood asked himself.

Because he could find no solution, when he returned to the house he was in a bad temper.

This resulted in his being cold and distant to Lalita when they met for dinner.

He knew she was looking at him pleadingly and that she wanted to ask him to forgive her if she had done anything wrong.

But it was impossible to talk intimately in the Dining-Room with Carter coming in and out with the dishes he had cooked, and when the meal was over instead of going into the Writing-Room as they usually did, Lord Heywood went off to the stables.

There were only the two horses to look at, and to his surprise they were not in the paddock, as he had expected, but in their stalls.

There was an excuse for Conqueror to be resting there, but why Waterloo?

He was patting the latter absent-mindedly while thinking about Lalita when Carter joined him.

"I wondered why you had the horses inside," Lord Heywood remarked.

"I thinks we're in for a thunderstorm, M'Lord."

"I would not be surprised," Lord Heywood replied, aware how stifling hot it was.

"There's been rumblings in th' distance all th' afternoon," Carter went on, "and I suspects they're havin' a storm not far from 'ere. If it reaches us, Waterloo'll be upset."

He grinned before he added:

" 'E'll think 'e's back on the battlefield, and 'e's bin a bit gun-shy ever since that six-pounder went off just beside you."

Lord Heywood remembered it well, and it had been only by a superb show of horsemanship that he had not been thrown from Waterloo's back.

"You are quite right to bring the horses in," he said approvingly. "We do not want any harm to come to our only means of conveyance."

As he spoke he was thinking that horses when they were frightened could easily impale themselves on a fence or try to jump a hedge that was too high for them.

When he walked back to the house, everything seemed quiet and he thought that Carter had perhaps been needlessly apprehensive.

Now lying in his bed and wearing nothing above the waist, he thought the thunderstorm would be a blessing and would clear the air, especially if it rained afterwards.

Even as he thought of it there was a streak of lightning which lit the whole room, followed by a resounding crash that appeared to be directly over the house.

It was so unexpected that Lord Heywood felt himself start. Then he lay looking through the open window, waiting for the next.

It was not long in coming, first the lightning, then an even louder clap of thunder, followed by another crash which certainly shook the open windows if not the whole house.

Then he heard a door open and turned to see indistinctly in the darkness somebody wearing white, standing inside the communicating door which led between his room and the one which had been his mother's.

"Lalita!" he exclaimed.

As he spoke, a flash of lightning revealed her frightened face framed by her fair hair, and the blast which followed it was so loud that it was almost deafening.

The next thing Lord Heywood knew, Lalita was clinging to him and her face was hidden against his shoulder.

Wonderingly he put his arms round her, and because he had risen up slightly on the pillows when he saw her, he fell back against them so that she was lying beside him on the bed.

He could feel her trembling and also the warmth of her body through her diaphanous nightgown.

"It is all right," he said soothingly.

"I . . . I am afraid it will . . . hit the house," he heard her say incoherently.

As she spoke, lightning once again lit up the room and the thunder vibrated through it almost simultaneously.

Instinctively Lord Heywood tightened his arms and drew her closer still, and as he did so he realised that he loved her.

It was something he had known subconsciously for some time but had been determined not to admit it. Now, however, he knew that he loved her in a way that was different from anything he had felt before.

"W-will it . . . hurt us?" Lalita asked in a voice that trembled, and as she spoke her whole body seemed to quiver with fear.

As she raised her face to ask the question, a flash of lightning made Lord Heywood see her wide, frightened eyes looking at him, her face very pale and her lips parted.

He could only see her in the passing of a second, and yet it was enough to imprint her loveliness on his mind forever.

Because he could not help himself he turned towards her and his lips came down on hers.

For a moment Lalita could not believe it was happening, but suddenly her fear of the thunderstorm was gone, and Lord Heywood's lips and the strength of his arms swept everything from her mind except him.

She knew as he kissed her that this was what she had been wanting and longing for although she had not been aware of it.

The unhappiness she had felt because she thought he was angry with her was swept away by an inexpressible joy that seemed to rise within her and become a rapture that she had thought existed only in her dreams.

Lord Heywood's lips were at first fierce and possessive, then as if what she was feeling communicated itself to him, his mouth became more gentle.

The wonder of it was to Lalita so perfect that she thought she must be dreaming.

Then she was aware that it was no dream, that Lord Heywood was very real, and his arms encircled her as if

113

to protect her against everything else in the world, and his lips still held hers captive. . . .

A few minutes later he raised his head, and when she gave an inarticulate little murmur because she thought she had lost him, he said in a voice which she found hard to recognise:

"Oh, God, how can you do this to me?"

Then he was kissing her again.

He kissed her as if he was demanding that she surrender herself to him and at the same time wooing her so that she wanted to give him anything he desired.

'I am his . . . I have always . . . been his,' she thought.

Then it was hard to think because he was awakening in her sensations which she had no idea existed or which she was capable of feeling.

It was as if every nerve in her body vibrated to him, and at the same time she was a part of him and they were no longer two people but one.

He went on kissing her and they were neither of them aware that the thunder was gradually fading away into the distance.

Now the rain came pouring down tempestuously, bringing with it a freshness which lightened the air and dissipated the oppressive heat.

It was then that Lalita felt as if Lord Heywood had swept her into the sky and they left the earth behind. . . .

What might have been a long time later his lips released hers and he said hoarsely in a voice that was curiously unsteady:

"My darling, my precious, this is wrong and should not have happened."

"How . . . can it be . . . wrong?" Lalita asked. "It is wonderful . . . and I . . . love you!"

"And God knows I love you!" Lord Heywood replied. "But I have nothing to give you."

"You have . . . everything," Lalita replied, "everything I have ever . . . wanted or . . . dreamt of or . . . imagined I would ever . . . find."

She gave a little sound that was almost a sob as she added:

"I did not . . . know that . . . love could be so . . . wonderful."

"Nor did I," Lord Heywood said. "Nor have I ever loved anybody as I love you."

"Is that . . . true?"

"I want to convince you it is true," he said. "But, my precious, we have to be sensible."

"Why?" Lalita asked.

She felt apprehensively that he was going to say something she did not want to hear, and she put out her hand, groping for his face which she could see only very dimly in the faint light coming from the window.

"Is it . . . true that you . . . love me?" she asked.

"I love you, but I have a sense of propriety and perhaps decency," Lord Heywood replied. "What have I to offer you?"

"You are my whole . . . life and . . . everything I will ever . . . want," Lalita answered.

"Oh, my sweet, how can I be sure of that?" he asked.

He let her head fall back on the pillow; then, bending over, he was kissing her, first her lips, then her eyes, then the softness of her neck.

He knew as the breath came quickly from between her parted lips and her fingers tightened on his shoulder that he had aroused in her feelings that were very different from anything she had ever felt before.

Then suddenly he drew away from her to lie back against the pillows, breathing quickly and staring at the window.

The rain had stopped and now the sky was clearing and it was possible to see the stars.

"This is wrong!" Lord Heywood said. "But, my precious, I cannot help myself."

"Do you mean it is . . . wrong for you to love . . . me?" Lalita asked. "I do not believe anything that is . . . perfect, so glorious . . . and so much a . . . part of . . . God could be wrong."

He did not speak and she went on:

"I knew today when you were helping me clean the Chapel that you were noble and good and that no man could be so wonderful! But I did not even then . . . realise that what I was . . . feeling for you was . . . love."

She put out her hand to touch him as she said:

"Love can . . . never be wrong . . . I am sure of that."

"It is not our love that is wrong," Lord Heywood said, and she thought he was speaking with difficulty. "It is that I should not ask you to be my wife, knowing the privations you will suffer because of it."

"Do you . . . want me to be . . . your wife?" Lalita asked in a very small voice.

"Of course I want it!" he replied fiercely. "I want you to belong to me, to be mine for the rest of our lives together, and after that through all eternity."

He smiled before he added:

"This is the first time I have ever asked anybody to marry me, or wanted anybody I have known to be my wife, but I know now, my lovely one, instinctively I was waiting for you."

"I am so glad, so very, very glad," Lalita said. "Just

suppose when we met you had been . . . married to . . . somebody else?"

As she spoke she was thinking of Lady Irene, and Lord Heywood said sharply:

"Forget her! She shall not spoil our lives and I will not allow her to hurt you."

"Nothing can hurt me," Lalita said, "unless you . . . wish to leave . . . or send me . . . away."

She said the last words in a voice which told Lord Heywood that she was afraid that might happen.

"That is what I should do," he said, but not very positively.

"Nothing . . . nothing in the world could make me . . . leave you . . . now," Lalita said. "All I want is to stay here with you in the Abbey . . . and be happy for ever and ever . . . just like the fairy-stories."

"My precious!" Lord Heywood said.

He turned to her again, and now in the light of the stars he could see her face on the pillow, her eyes seeking his face.

"You are so beautiful!" he said. "So ridiculously, absurdly beautiful! If you went to London you would have every man at your feet, and you could marry somebody who could deck you in jewels, put a coronet on your head, and give you the life of comfort and luxury that your beauty deserves."

"But nobody could give me a house as perfect as this one," Lalita replied. "And no man except . . . you could give me . . . the stars round my heart and the sun to warm me . . . every day of our lives . . . together."

The way she spoke made Lord Heywood feel as if he were listening to music, and he said in a voice which told her he was very moved:

"What have I done to deserve you?"

As he spoke he drew his finger along her little winged eye-brows and down the straightness of her nose. Then he outlined her lips, first the top of them and then the bottom, knowing as he did so that once again she was quivering as he had made her do when he had kissed her neck.

"I love . . . you!" she whispered. "And when you do . . . that I want to . . . kiss you . . . and kiss . . . you and . . . feel you hold me very . . . very . . . close."

"My darling, I have so much to teach you."

Then he was kissing her again, and it seemed to Lalita that it was impossible to feel so ecstatically happy without dying from the wonder of it.

Suddenly Lord Heywood stopped kissing her and, moving away, slipped off the bed and on the other side.

As he did so he picked up a long silk robe which lay on one of the chairs, put it on, then walked to the window to stand looking out with his back to Lalita.

Now he could see the garden clearly in the starlight and there was the fragrance of the freshness after rain.

As he stood there getting back his breath, he heard a little voice behind him say:

"Have I . . . have I . . . done anything . . . wrong?"

Lord Heywood made a sound that was half a laugh and yet a very strange one, before he turned and came back to the bed to sit down beside Lalita, facing her.

He could see her more clearly now and he thought that nobody could look more lovely and at the same time insubstantial, as if he had imagined her in his dreams and by some magic she had become reality.

He realised that she was looking at him anxiously, and her hands went out to him apprehensively.

"Everything you do is wonderful and perfect," he said, "but, my darling, I am a man and when you excite me so tremendously it is difficult to remember that I must also behave like a gentleman."

"Do I really . . . excite . . . you?" Lalita asked.

"Far too much for us to continue to live like this," he replied. "How soon will you marry me?"

She gave a little cry of sheer delight.

"You will marry me . . . you will . . . really?"

"If you swear that you love me enough, that you will never regret it or accuse me of taking advantage of you."

"If you will not marry me," Lalita said, "I should only want to . . . die, because there will be nothing . . . left to . . . live for."

Her fingers tightened on his.

"How could I . . . lose you? How could I lose the . . . happiness I have never . . . known before, which is so wonderful . . . so perfect that being . . . married to you will be like . . . living in . . . Paradise."

"I hope you will always think that."

"I will try very . . . very . . . hard to make you as . . . happy as I . . . am."

"My precious, that is what I should be saying to you," Lord Heywood answered.

He could see the happiness in her face and a faint reflection of the starlight in her eyes as she looked at him.

He knew too that her hand was pulling him towards her and she wanted him to kiss her again.

With a superhuman effort he controlled his desire to hold her close to him.

"Listen, my lovely one," he said, "you must go back to bed. Tomorrow I will send Carter to London to obtain a Special Licence, and as soon as he returns I will ask the local Parson, whom I remember, to marry us here in the Chapel."

Lalita gave a cry of excitement and sat up.

"That is what I would like above all else," she said, "and we will decorate the Chapel with flowers. Although it will be a secret marriage, no bride could feel more sanctified or have a more perfect wedding."

"And no bridegroom could have a more beautiful bride."

"It will be very . . . very . . . wonderful!" Lalita murmured.

Then she exclaimed:

"I wish the night would pass quickly so we could tell Carter to start off for London immediately."

"You are no more impatient than I am," Lord Heywood said.

His eyes were on her lips as he rose to his feet and drew her to hers.

Now he could see how slender she was through the almost transparent nightgown, and it was with an effort that she would not have understood that he restrained himself from holding her close to him again.

Instead he drew her across the room to the communicating door through which she had come to him and they walked through it into the other bedroom.

All the curtains were drawn but Lord Heywood lit a candle by the bedside and as he did so Lalita slid between the sheets.

The room smelt of roses and there was a big vase of them which Lalita had put on a table between the windows, and Lord Heywood knew that the same scent had come from her hair when he had kissed her.

He thought that with her innocence and purity she was like one of the white rose-trees which grew in profusion in the rose-garden and which had been one of his mother's favourite flowers.

He sat down beside her on the bed to look at her and

knew in the light of the candle that it was impossible for anybody to look more beautiful and yet untouched.

There was something young and spring-like about Lalita that made him know he must protect her always, even against himself.

"I love you, my precious one!" he said in his deep voice. "And when we are married I will be able to tell you how overwhelmingly I want you. But we must wait until we are blessed by God for you to belong to me."

He spoke gently and quietly and there was a serious note in his voice which told Lalita that she must try to understand what he was saying to her.

As if he sensed that she was a little bewildered, he added with a smile:

"What I am saying, my darling, is that you must not come to my room as you did tonight until my wedding-ring is on your finger, unless of course something frightens you."

Lalita smiled at him.

"Perhaps it may have been . . . unconventional . . . and even a little . . . improper," she said, "but I am not sorry. If I had not come . . . perhaps you would . . . never have told me that you . . . love me."

This was undoubtedly true, and Lord Heywood could only appreciate the quickness of her thinking.

"Eventually," he said, "I should have found it impossible not to kiss you. The thunderstorm of course was a perfect excuse, but it is something I have wanted to do for a very long time."

"You . . . did want to . . . kiss me?"

"You are a very kissable person, my sweet."

"Then please . . . kiss me now."

She held up her arms as she spoke, and Lord Heywood pulled her quickly against him, his arms went round her, and his lips found hers.

It was a quick kiss, then he released her and sat up.

"Go to sleep, my little love," he said firmly, "and tomorrow, as you have said, we will start getting everything ready for our wedding. Until then, I am going to behave as your mother would expect me to do."

"I am sure too that your mother knows how . . . happy we . . . are," Lalita said, "and I know she would . . . want me to . . . look after you and . . . love you."

"As I will look after you."

He bent forward and kissed her once again, a very gentle kiss.

Then he blew out the light.

"Good-night, my darling wife-to-be," he said. "Dream of me."

"How could I dream of anyone else?" Lalita asked.

She heard the communicating door between their rooms close and felt that she wanted to run after him and tell him once again how much she loved him.

Then she knew she must behave as he wanted her to do.

As she snuggled down against the pillows she could think only of the wonder of his kisses and the glorious feelings he had awakened in her, and the incredible, marvellous happiness they would find together.

"How could I have been so lucky, so incredibly fortunate, as to find such a wonderful, magnificent man?" she asked in the darkness.

Then she was thanking God so fervently that her words fell over themselves as she said over and over again:

"Thank You, God . . . for giving me . . . love . . . thank You for . . . letting me . . . find love with a man who is so . . . perfect that he might have . . . come from Heaven itself!"

*   *   *

It was impossible to sleep once dawn had broken, and because the sun was shining Lalita could not bear to miss one second of the day when she might be with Lord Heywood.

She wondered if perhaps he might be tired after being awake so late, and while she was thinking about him she heard the door of his room close and his footsteps pass her door, and she knew he was already dressed.

Quickly she jumped out of bed, and while she wished to hurry, woman-like because she was in love, she took longer in arranging her hair and dressing than she would have done on an ordinary day.

Then she sped downstairs wearing the habit that had belonged to Lord Heywood's mother.

As it was too hot for the jacket she only wore a pretty white muslin blouse inset with lace that made her look very young and little more than a School-Girl.

When she entered the Breakfast-Room, Lord Heywood felt as if the sunshine came in with her.

He rose from the table in the window in which he was sitting, and as she ran to his side to stand looking up at him, her eyes seemed to fill her whole face.

"You slept?" he asked.

"I dreamt of you . . . as you told . . . me to do."

Lalita's voice was very low. Then she asked:

"It was . . . true last night? You did say you . . . loved me?"

"I love you!"

There was no need for either of them to say any more.

Their love vibrated between them, and although he

had not touched her, Lalita felt as if she were in his arms and his lips were on hers.

Then Carter came into the room and broke the spell, but whether he was there or not, words seemed unnecessary, and every minute or so one of them forgot to eat as they looked at each other across the table.

After breakfast, when Lord Heywood told Carter that he required a Special Licence, he knew by the expression on his face that it was no surprise.

"Congratulations, M'Lord!" Carter said. "An' if you asks me, it's the best possible thing Your Lordship's ever done. Miss Lalita'd be just the wife I'd choose for you, if you'd asked me."

Lord Heywood laughed.

It was the sort of thing which only Carter would say.

"I am glad it pleases you, Carter."

"It does, M'Lord!" Carter replied. "An' Miss Lalita could no more manage on her own than a babe in arms, so we can see she comes to no trouble here with us."

"Yes, Carter, we will make certain of that," Lord Heywood said.

It was only when Carter was ready to leave and Lord Heywood realised that he must write down their names for the Special Licence that he said to Lalita:

"It seems absurd, my darling, and no-one would believe it, but I do not know your name."

"It is . . . Duncan."

She said it in a way which told Lord Heywood that she expected him to recognise it, but although he tried to remember any association with that name, for the moment his mind was blank.

"Surely," he said, "it is about time you told me your momentous secret?"

"It is a . . . long story and we . . . have so . . .

much to do . . . today," Lalita replied. "Please, can it . . . wait until tonight?"

"If that is what you want," Lord Heywood replied.

She looked so lovely that he thought he would try to give her the moon if she asked him for it, and her secret was not important now that they loved each other.

He did not realise that Lalita was thinking frantically that she could not, dared not, tell him her secret until they were married.

"Tonight I will make some . . . excuse," she decided, "then once we are married there will be nothing he . . . can do, however . . . angry it makes him."

When Carter had left, Lord Heywood and Lalita went out riding.

They decided not to do anything too strenuous because Conqueror was tired after two days of long journeys, and as Carter had taken Waterloo to London, Lalita rode the horse from the farm.

But they were quite content to move slowly through the woods where it was shadowy, talking to each other, or just happy to be side by side and knowing they communicated without words.

Back at the Abbey, they went once again to work in the Chapel. There were two little birds fluttering round the ceiling when they entered it, and Lord Heywood looking up at them said:

"We shall have to try to find somebody who will put in a few panes of glass, although I suppose it would be cheaper if I climbed up on a ladder and covered the holes with paper."

"Do you think you should do that?" Lalita asked.

"Of course," he replied. "I hope you realize by now that I am very handy about the house."

"I think you could do anything you wanted to," Lalita said. "I told you, you always win."

"I have won the only thing in life that matters to me," he said, "and that is you."

They looked at each other, but as they were in the Chapel Lord Heywood did not kiss her.

He merely started once again to sweep the flagged floor while Lalita polished the rail across the Chancel and the candlesticks which they had found thrown down at the back of the altar and which had become almost black with neglect.

Only when they paused because it was luncheon-time did Lalita ask:

"Do you think Carter will really be back this afternoon?"

"He assured me he would be here in time to cook our dinner," Lord Heywood replied.

"Then can we be married tomorrow?" Lalita asked.

"Why not?" Lord Heywood enquired.

He saw by the radiance on her face how much the idea excited her.

Then she pulled off the apron she was wearing over a pretty muslin gown which had belonged to his mother and they walked back from the Chapel along the corridor which led to the main house.

They had reached the Hall when they both heard the sound of wheels outside the front door.

Lalita looked at Lord Heywood uncertainly.

"It must be somebody calling on you," she said quickly. "Shall I hide?"

"Certainly not!" he replied. "We will stick to our story and say we are married."

He walked towards the front door, which Carter had left open as it was so hot.

A man was coming up the steps and behind him

there was a Phaeton in which another man was picking up the reins as if he had just sat down in the driver's seat.

As Lord Heywood had a quick impression of this he suddenly heard Lalita give a little cry, and as the man walked into the Hall she exclaimed in a voice that was barely audible:

"Uncle . . . Edward!"

The man who had simultaneously seen her was, Lord Heywood thought, a gentleman but an unpleasant-looking one.

He had a long nose and eyes that appeared to be too close together, and there was something dissolute and distinctly unattractive about him.

"So here you are!" the newcomer said. "And the last place I should have expected to find you. Yet when Lady Irene Dawlish came to the Manor to shelter from the storm and described the woman her paramour had married, I felt I was not mistaken."

While Lalita was obviously speechless and Lord Heywood could feel her trembling beside him, he moved a step in front of her to say:

"As you have not introduced yourself, I should be glad to know your name. Mine, as I imagine you already know, is Heywood!"

"And mine, as I expect you are aware, is Edward Duncan!" was the reply. "Although, Lord Heywood, you may think you have been very clever, I consider you to be a dirty, sneaking fortune-hunter, and you are not going to get away with it!"

He spoke with such violence that Lord Heywood stared at him in astonishment.

"If you imagine," Lalita's uncle went on, his voice rising with fury, "that you can abduct an heiress and marry her without her Guardian's permission, you are mistaken!"

"No . . . no, Uncle Edward!" Lalita cried, moving towards him. "What you are saying is . . . untrue! Lord Heywood has no idea that I . . . have a fortune! He . . . married me because we are . . . in love with each other . . . and there is . . . nothing you can do . . . about it!"

"There is everything I can do, and everything I intend to do!" Edward Duncan said. "No Court, I can tell you, will believe that 'Heywood the Penniless' is not well aware that with your fortune you are the answer to his problem of how to keep up the house and pay off his father's debts!"

Edward Duncan's sneering voice rose as he went on:

"Come, I am taking you away. Your marriage will be termed invalid and you will then marry Philip as I intended you should do in the first place."

"I will not . . . marry Philip . . . or anybody . . . else!" Lalita cried.

Edward Duncan reached out his left hand to grasp her wrist, and as Lord Heywood stepped forward to intervene he drew a pistol from his pocket.

"Now keep back, Heywood," he said, "or I will shoot you down where you stand! I am taking my niece away with me and you can try to substantiate your claim later. In the meantime, Lalita is coming with me, and I advise you not to try to prevent it."

"I will not . . . go with . . . you! I . . . refuse!" Lalita cried.

"You will leave Lalita here," Lord Heywood said sharply.

"Why should I?" Edward Duncan asked. "You have committed an illegal act, Heywood, and if you interfere I will have you transported for abducting a minor!"

As he spoke he was dragging Lalita through the front door. She was resisting him, but he was very strong and pulled her forward despite every effort she made to prevent him from doing so.

"I insist that you hear what I have to say," Lord Heywood said.

He had followed them out through the front door and was standing at the top of the steps, while Edward Duncan had already started to descend, dragging Lalita after him.

"Stand back or you will be sorry!" he shouted.

As he spoke he jerked Lalita's arm, and because she was still pulling against him, her foot slipped and she staggered and fell forward.

As she did so, Lord Heywood leapt onto Edward Duncan.

He went down with a crash on the steps, and the weight of Lord Heywood's body cracked his head violently against the edge of one of the stone steps.

It knocked him unconscious and the pistol fell from his hand with a clatter.

Lord Heywood got to his feet, then picked the unconscious man up in his arms and carried him down the remaining steps to the side of the Phaeton.

He flung him on the floor of the vehicle and said to the man holding the reins:

"Take that swine away and make sure he does not come back!"

"You have no right to treat my father in such a way!" the man replied nervously.

"If he is your father, then I am sorry for you," Lord Heywood retorted. "Now get off my land, and the quicker the better!"

He spoke in a tone which apparently frightened Philip Duncan into obeying him.

He brought the whip down hard on his horses and they leapt forward, with one of Edward Duncan's legs dangling out of the Phaeton as he lay unconscious at his son's feet.

Lord Heywood watched them go, then he bent down and picked up the pistol which lay on the bottom step, and turned to see Lalita standing above him.

She was very pale and obviously frightened.

"You . . . saved . . . me!" she cried. "I . . . thought he would . . . take me . . . away!"

She sounded not far from tears, but the expression on Lord Heywood's face, she saw apprehensively, was neither compassionate nor tender.

Holding the pistol in his hand, he walked up the steps.

When he was level with her he said, and she thought his voice was grim:

"I think you have a lot of explaining to do, Lalita, and I want to hear the truth—now!"

Chapter Seven

Lord Heywood walked across the Hall and into the Writing-Room.

Lalita followed him, wondering frantically if everything she had planned had gone wrong and now she would lose all that mattered to her in the world.

She shut the door of the Writing-Room behind her and stood looking at Lord Heywood, her eyes filling her whole face and mirroring her apprehension.

She was still trembling a little from her terror of being taken away by her uncle, and she wanted to run to Lord Heywood and hide her face against his shoulder and feel his arms go round her.

Without looking at her he said:

"I think I remember now a General Duncan who lived about six miles from here."

"That was my grandfather."

"He commanded the Coldstream Regiment?"

"Yes."

"Why did you not tell me about him?"

"Grandpapa was dead, and you have seen Uncle Edward! As I told you, he was . . . determined to . . . marry me to his son . . . Philip."

"Because you are an heiress?"

Lalita walked a little nearer to him. Then, because she felt as if she might fall down, she seated herself on the edge of one of the arm-chairs.

"At first," she said in a very small voice, "I was . . . afraid you would send me . . . back. Then when you were so . . . insistent that you would not . . . accept money from . . . a woman, I could not . . . tell you that I was . . . wealthy."

Lord Heywood did not speak, and Lalita cried out as if she could not prevent the words coming from her lips:

"Please . . . please marry me! Now that I . . . love you . . . I could not go away and live alone . . . and surely love . . . is more important than . . . money?"

She clasped her hands together as she spoke and the tears came into her eyes with the intensity of her feelings.

Lord Heywood did not look at her as he said:

"You told me this morning that you would tell me the whole story tonight. Is that what you would have done?"

Lalita could not answer him and after a moment he said:

"I have the idea that actually you intended to marry me without letting me be aware that you are an heiress."

As this was the truth Lalita could not deny it, and after a moment she said still in a small, frightened voice:

"Shall I tell you what . . . actually . . . happened?"

"That is what I wish to know."

"My father met my mother, who was American and came from the South, when she was in England on a visit. They fell very . . . very much in . . . love with . . . each other."

Lalita's voice softened on the last words and she

looked appealingly at Lord Heywood as if she felt that what she was saying must mean something to him.

He did not speak and she went on:

"They were married, but it was sometime after the war with the French had started, and it was too dangerous for Mama to journey back to America, and anyway Papa was in the Coldstream Guards."

"So she stayed in England and you were born here," Lord Heywood said.

Lalita nodded.

"I think even Papa forgot that Mama was American, and although she wrote to her father and mother, the letters were often delayed for a long time, and when much later England was actually at war with America they ceased altogether."

"I can understand that," Lord Heywood remarked.

"Then Papa was wounded in the leg and invalided out of the Regiment," Lalita went on, "and as Grandmama had died and Grandpapa was retired, we went to live with him at the Manor House where I have been ever since."

"Where is it exactly?"

"At Little Sheldon. It is a very small village."

"I remember it now," Lord Heywood remarked.

"It is about six miles from here by road," Lalita said, "but a very much shorter distance if one rides across country."

There was just a faint smile on Lord Heywood's lips as he said:

"I imagine that is how you knew so much about my Estate."

"I used to ride here to look at the house," Lalita said, "and because it was beautiful I used to tell myself stories about it. When your grandfather died . . . I wondered what . . . you were . . . like."

She paused and after a moment Lord Heywood said: "Go on!"

"After Waterloo, when hostilities had ceased, Mama received a letter from America to say that her father was dead and had left her all his money."

"He was a rich man?" Lord Heywood asked.

"Very rich," Lalita said, "and as it was important that Mama should go and see what she now owned, she and Papa set off, leaving me with Grandpapa."

"Was that about two years ago?" Lord Heywood asked.

"As it was in August, it was a little under two years ago."

"What happened?"

"The ship in which they were returning . . . foundered and . . . everybody on board was . . . drowned."

Lalita's voice broke and Lord Heywood took a step forward, then checked himself.

With what he thought was a superhuman effort at self-control Lalita went on:

"Mama had already written to Grandpapa telling him how much . . . money she had . . . inherited and explaining that as I was her only child it would all . . . eventually come to . . . me."

"And what did your grandfather think about that?"

"He was not very pleased," Lalita answered. "He said to me: 'This means you will have every damned fortune-hunter in England knocking on your door! So to make sure that does not happen, we will say nothing whatever about it.' "

"Your grandfather was wise, and when he died I presume that was where your Uncle Edward took over?"

"That is exactly what did happen," Lalita agreed. "I suppose Grandpapa's Solicitors must have told him, for he arrived at the Manor saying he was my Guardian and I must do what he told me to do."

"Had you seen much of him before that?"

"No, because Grandpapa had never approved of him, firstly because he would not join the Regiment and fight during the war, with the excuse that he was not well enough to do so, and secondly because he was very extravagant and was always asking Grandpapa to pay his debts."

"I can understand why your grandfather had no wish for him to know about you."

"Grandpapa did not wish . . . anybody to know. He intended this year to take me to London and let me go to some of the Balls and parties, but he was taken ill and so all our plans had to be postponed."

"Did you mind very much?"

"No, I was quite happy at the Manor. I had horses to ride, lots of pretty gowns, and if Grandpapa was frightened of fortune-hunters, so was I!"

"But you must have wanted to get married?"

"Only if I fell . . . in love."

Lalita gave a little cry as she added:

"Can you imagine what I felt when Uncle Edward brought Philip with him to the Manor and told me we were to be . . . married? I think that he had learnt from the Solicitors, who had been in touch with the Trustees of my grandfather's Estate in America, that the only way he could get control of my money was if I married . . . his son."

Lord Heywood was certain that this was indeed the truth, and he said:

"Then because you were frightened of your uncle and of having to marry your cousin you ran away."

"I was very . . . very . . . frightened," Lalita said. "I felt that Uncle Edward would stop at . . . nothing to force me to . . . marry Philip, so I came. . . . here."

Lord Heywood thought it was in fact rather clever of

her to have reckoned that few people would suspect she would hide herself away in an empty house where there was nobody to look after her and she would obviously have difficulty in providing herself with food.

As if she could read his thoughts, Lalita said:

"Then . . . you came home . . . and everything has been so . . . wonderful and I have never . . . known such . . . happiness!"

She rose to her feet and moved towards Lord Heywood.

"You cannot send me . . . away now," she said pleadingly. "You cannot . . . refuse to . . . marry me. You need not use my money, you can just forget about it but I . . . cannot live . . . without you!"

The tears were back in her eyes and her voice was almost incoherent.

Lord Heywood looked at her and slowly his arms went out towards her.

She gave a little cry and flung herself against him.

As she did so the door of the Writing-Room opened and a man's voice said:

"Excuse me, but as I found it impossible to make anybody hear me either by ringing the bell or by knocking at the door, I came in."

Both Lalita and Lord Heywood turned to look at the intruder in surprise.

He was a short, grey-haired man wearing glasses and he looked like a respectable School-Master.

Lord Heywood took his arms from Lalita and walked towards the newcomer.

"I am afraid my servant is out, but I am Lord Heywood. Were you wishing to see me?"

"Yes indeed, My Lord, and I must apologise for my intrusion and for arriving unannounced."

"Who are you?"

"My name is Walton, My Lord. I have come to see you on the instructions of Messrs. Christie, the Auctioneers, and I am their Valuer."

"Of course!" Lord Heywood exclaimed. "I asked them to send one, but I was not expecting you to arrive so quickly!"

"I am aware of that, My Lord, but as my business with Your Lordship was very urgent, I came down from London last night, having just missed you after you had left Heywood House."

"Come and sit down," Lord Heywood said, "and tell me why your business is so urgent. I did ask the Partner I spoke to at Christie's to send somebody down as soon as possible, but I expected them to inspect Heywood House before they came here."

"That is what I have to explain to Your Lordship," Mr. Walton said.

As he spoke he walked forward and sat down on the nearest chair, a brief-case in his hand.

Lalita, who had been surreptitiously wiping her tears from her eyes, now sat on the other side of the fireplace while Lord Heywood stood with his back to it.

"I came as far as the next village last night," Mr. Walton said conversationally. "I was hoping to reach Your Lordship immediately after breakfast this morning, but I was involved on my way here in a very nasty accident."

"An accident?" Lord Heywood questioned.

"Yes, My Lord. I met a Phaeton driven in a crazy manner by a young man who had no control over his horses. In an effort to avoid the Post-Chaise in which I was travelling, he crashed into the narrow bridge on the outskirts of your village."

As he spoke, Lalita rose from where she was sitting to stand beside Lord Heywood.

"What happened?" Lord Heywood enquired.

"It was all very unpleasant, My Lord," Mr. Walton replied. "The Phaeton turned against the corner of the bridge and an elderly man who was also travelling in it was thrown into the stream below."

Mr. Walton paused to take his spectacles from his eyes and polish the lenses with his handkerchief.

As if she could not bear the suspense, Lalita put her hand on Lord Heywood's arm and he covered it with his.

"Was the man who was thrown into the water injured?" he asked quietly.

"I regret to tell you, My Lord," Mr. Walton replied, "that by the time the body, which had floated downstream, was recovered, the gentleman was dead!"

Lalita's lips parted but no sound came from them.

Mr. Walton put his spectacles back on his nose.

"There was nothing I could do," he said, "and as the Vicar and several sensible-looking villagers appeared, I drove on, as I was anxious to see Your Lordship as quickly as possible."

Lalita gave a deep sigh and Lord Heywood knew it was one of relief.

If her uncle was dead, then the trouble he could have caused them no longer existed.

Lalita's eyes as she looked up at Lord Heywood were very revealing, and as he smiled at her she felt as if the sun enveloped them both and the darkness had gone.

His fingers on hers were also very comforting.

Mr. Walton, quite unaware of the sensation he had unknowingly caused, was opening his brief-case.

"After you left Christie's a few days ago, My Lord," he said, "a Senior Partner was informed that the Ambassador of a country which for the moment must remain anonymous had presented us with a rather unusual assignment."

"What was that?" Lord Heywood asked.

"This country, which will have a very much more significant role in European affairs since the Congress of Vienna, wishes to build a new Embassy in London. They told us that as its completion will take several years, they wish in the meantime to rent an imposing house in which they can conduct their country's business."

There was a sudden glint of excitement in Lord Heywood's eyes, but he said nothing as Mr. Walton went on slowly and rather pompously:

"The Partners of Christie's, My Lord, could think of no house more suitable than your own, if Your Lordship would be prepared to let it, at what I am told is a very generous rent, exactly as it stands."

"By that you mean with all its contents," Lord Heywood said.

"The Partner to whom Your Lordship spoke a few days ago gathered that Heywood House is ready, as one might say, for occupation, and that would be a considerable convenience both to the tenants and to my firm."

"I am certainly prepared to let Heywood House as it stands," Lord Heywood said.

He tried to speak dispassionately, but he could not prevent a slightly eager note from creeping into his voice.

"That is a very great relief, My Lord," Mr. Walton replied. "I have here a draft Lease for Your Lordship's perusal, which of course you would wish to show to your Solicitors before signing."

"Of course," Lord Heywood agreed.

Then, as if he felt that in some way he must celebrate this unexpected good fortune, he said:

Barbara Cartland

"I must apologise, Mr. Walton, for not offering you some refreshment. It is what I am sure you need after your traumatic experience on your way here."

"Thank you, My Lord," Mr. Walton replied. "It was, I admit, a trifle upsetting."

"What would you like?" Lord Heywood enquired. "A glass of sherry?"

Mr. Walton shook his head.

"I am afraid, My Lord, I am a teetotaller. Alcohol, I find, disagrees with me."

Lord Heywood looked at Lalita.

"I am sure what Mr. Walton would enjoy," he said, "is a glass of your peach-juice."

"Yes, of course," she replied.

Her eyes were shining and for the moment she could think of nothing but the joy of knowing that if Lord Heywood could let his house in London he would not feel he was entirely dependent on her money.

As she left the Writing-Room and ran along the passage, her heart was singing and she was saying a little prayer of gratitude:

"Thank You, God, thank You! I am sure now he will not refuse to marry me."

As she reached the kitchen she remembered she had put the peach-juice down in the cellar to keep cool.

She ran down the stone steps, picked up the pitcher from the flagged floor, then hesitated for a moment, wondering if she should also bring a bottle of wine for Lord Heywood.

Then she was sure that however much he would wish to celebrate, he would not wish to drink so early in the morning.

Instead she carried the heavy pitcher carefully back to the Writing-Room, anxious not to upset its contents.

When she entered the room Lord Heywood was

140

sitting at his desk with some papers in front of him and Mr. Walton was standing beside him.

"It all seems very clear," Lord Heywood was saying, "I really see no reason why I should not sign it immediately."

As he spoke he was thinking that he had no desire to go to London again and leave Lalita.

"I assure you, My Lord," Mr. Walton said, "it is a very fair lease which will benefit both our clients and Your Lordship."

"I am aware of that," Lord Heywood said.

As Lalita crossed the room he looked up and said:

"I will just read it through again. Have a drink of this very delicious fruit-juice. It is made from the peaches in the garden. I am sure that like me you will think it is unusual and very refreshing."

"I do not believe I have ever tasted peach-juice before," Mr. Walton said.

Lalita had taken a tumbler from the tray in the corner of the room and now she put it down on the desk and tipped some juice from the pitcher into it.

Mr. Walton watched her and only as the glass was nearly full did he suddenly exclaim:

"Where did you find that pitcher?"

He spoke so loudly that both Lalita and Lord Heywood started, then stared at him in astonishment.

"I cannot believe it!" Mr. Walton went on. "It must be a fake! But if it is, it is a very good one."

As he spoke he put out his hand across the desk to touch the pitcher which was in Lalita's hands.

Then he came round beside her to take it from her.

"I cannot believe it!" he said again. "I just cannot believe it!"

"What are you saying?" Lord Heywood asked.

As he spoke, both he and Lalita were looking at the pitcher, realising that they had hardly noticed it before.

It was a large pitcher in an ordinary shape with a handle and was decorated in what Lalita thought was a rather ugly geometric design in reddish-brown and black.

It had a certain glaze about it, but Lalita thought that otherwise there was nothing very distinctive to make Mr. Walton so excited.

Now he was running his fingers over the outside of the pitcher until finally he said:

"I am sure it is authentic, and I should think it is one of the best examples in existence!"

"Examples of what?" Lord Heywood enquired.

"Athenian Geometric pottery made about 750 B.C."

Lalita gave a cry.

"Do you mean that it is valuable?"

"Very, very valuable," Mr. Walton replied, "and it is madness for it to be used, as you appear to be doing, as an ordinary jug!"

Lalita looked at Lord Heywood.

"I think," he said, "Mr. Walton will be happier if the peach-juice is placed in some more ordinary vessel."

"I would indeed!" Mr. Walton said.

Lalita was not listening.

Instead she said breathlessly:

"I know this is not included in the Inventory."

"No, there is nothing listed which is Greek," Lord Heywood replied.

As he spoke he pulled open the drawer of his desk and took out the Inventory which they had carried round the house when they were trying to find something that could be sold.

Then as he put it down on the desk he said:

"I remember my grandfather went to Greece when

he was quite old, and I believe this Inventory was made before what was actually his last journey."

"In which case," Lalita said quickly, "there may be other things in the house!"

"Other things?" Mr. Walton enquired, his voice rising. "Do you mean to say there are other pieces of pottery as good as this?"

"I am afraid I really do not know," Lord Heywood admitted. "But we can certainly look. Where did you find this, Lalita?"

"It was in the Flower-Room with the vases."

Mr. Walton gave what was almost a groan of horror.

"It might easily have been broken," he said with a note of deep concern.

Lord Heywood rose to his feet.

"I think the best thing we can do," he said, "is to have a look at the Flower-Room."

"It is something I am very eager to do, My Lord," Mr. Walton said.

As he spoke he placed the pitcher for safety in the very centre of the desk.

"To think Your Lordship did not realise the value of this exquisite piece of Grecian pottery! It makes me shudder to think what might have happened to it!"

"Let us see if there is anything else being treated in such a casual manner," Lord Heywood said.

He was speaking to Mr. Walton, but his eyes met Lalita's and she slipped her hand into his. As she felt him squeeze her fingers there was no need for words. They were both thinking the same thing.

With Mr. Walton following them, they walked down the passage to what was known as the Flower-Room, which was situated near the Pantry.

It was the small room in which Lalita had found all

143

the vases used for flowers placed on narrow shelves round the walls.

In the centre there was a deal-table on which flowers could be arranged, and when she had wanted a jug in which to put the peach-juice she had simply taken the pitcher from one of the lower shelves.

When they entered the small room they stood back to let Mr. Walton look round.

He walked eagerly from shelf to shelf, and Lalita thought he was rather disappointed, until he gave an exclamation of excitement and lifted down what appeared to be a rather ordinary round bowl.

Almost reverently Mr. Walton said, and it sounded rather like an incantation:

"Longquan Celadon lotus-petal bowl, Song Dynasty!"

"You mean it is Chinese?" Lalita said.

"A perfect example," he said. "Look at the pale green glaze."

He was almost ecstatic over his find, and when the last shelf in the room produced a pottery jar with black and brown glaze which he said was from the Northern Song Dynasty, he was again so excited that Lalita did not like to say that she thought it rather ugly.

"I think the Chinese bowls belonged to my grandmother," Lord Heywood said ruminantly, "which is why they are not listed in the Inventory. I vaguely remember her telling me that her father had visited China."

"How could I have guessed they were so rare?" Lalita asked.

She thought Mr. Walton looked almost contemptuous of her ignorance, but nothing mattered except the satisfaction that she knew without words what Lord Heywood was feeling.

After Mr. Walton had begged them most earnestly to

place the Chinese bowls and the pitcher in a place of the utmost safety, he announced that he must return to London.

"You would not like to stay to luncheon?" Lord Heywood asked. "I am afraid it will be a very simple meal as my servant is not here, but you have brought me such good news that I would like to offer you some sort of hospitality."

"It is most gracious of Your Lordship," Mr. Walton replied, "but it is imperative that I return with the Lease, so that the Partners can inform their clients of Your Lordship's very welcome decision regarding Heywood House."

"It is no less welcome to me," Lord Heywood said, "and I would like to thank you most sincerely for finding these treasures, which I wish you to sell as soon as possible."

"I know Christie's will be overjoyed to be entrusted with three objects which will excite Curators everywhere."

"Why not take them with you?" Lord Heywood suggested.

Mr. Walton looked horrified.

"I would not take the responsibility, My Lord!" he replied quickly. "With Your Lordship's permission, I will send proper packers with a much more suitable vehicle than a Post-Chaise in which to convey them to London."

"Perhaps you are wise," Lord Heywood said. "To break them now after so many centuries would certainly be a disaster!"

Mr. Walton was so horrified at the idea that Lalita felt it was almost cruel to upset him.

As he disposed of the signed Lease of Heywood House in his brief-case, he said farewell with a new vitality which made Lalita think that he was longing to return to London and claim the credit for his finds.

After admonishing them once again to take as much care as possible of such unique treasures, Mr. Walton drove off.

Only as they stood at the top of the steps watching his Post-Chaise speeding up the drive did Lalita realise what Mr. Walton's visit meant.

She looked up at Lord Heywood and saw that the grimness had gone from his face, his eyes were shining, and she thought that in some strange way he looked immeasurably younger.

For a moment they stood looking at each other. Then Lord Heywood put out his arms and drew her against him.

"I think you are a witch!" he said. "You told me everything would come right and it has!"

"You have won!" Lalita said softly.

"I cannot believe it," he replied, "after all the worry and the sleepless nights, when I could see no possible way of solving our problem! Now I have rent my London house at what seems to me a very generous rate, and there will be more from the sale of our strange-looking pottery."

Lalita laughed.

"I thought that all three were rather ugly, and I do not regret in the very least your losing them, although I suppose I should not say so."

"Certainly not," Lord Heywood said firmly. "It would merely convince those who know that we have no taste."

"I still cannot . . . believe it," Lalita said. "Suppose we wake up and find they are just part of a dream and I have to go back to the . . . Manor and . . . Uncle Edward?"

Lord Heywood drew her closer to him.

"We are both of us so lucky, so unbelievably lucky!"

Lalita moved closer still.

"When . . . Carter comes . . . back . . ." she began hesitatingly.

Lord Heywood knew what she was asking, and there was a smile on his lips and a very tender one as he replied:

"I suppose now that you have no Guardian I will have to marry you, and you have hopelessly compromised yourself by staying here alone with me."

Lalita put her head against his shoulder.

"You do not . . . have to marry me," she whispered, "if you would really . . . prefer to be free."

"Then what do you suggest I do with you?" he asked.

"I could stay . . . here with you," she replied, "and if you are . . . ashamed of me . . . when your smart friends come to . . . visit you . . . I could always . . . hide . . . as I offered to do before."

Lord Heywood laughed and it was a very happy sound.

"You know quite well that I want what you want," he said, "and now we can put things on a very much more traditional basis."

Lalita looked up at him in a puzzled fashion and he went on:

"What I am saying, my precious darling, is that I can now ask you to marry me with a clear conscience! So will you, my adorable one, do me the very great honour of becoming my wife?"

There was so much seriousness in his voice as he said the last words that Lalita put her arms round his neck.

"That is what I wanted you to say!" she cried. "And you know the answer . . . Yes! Yes! Yes!"

"I believe if you behaved correctly," Lord Heywood

teased, "you would look shy and coy and would say: 'This is so sudden!' "

"If I did, I might give you a chance to escape," Lalita retorted. "Oh, my marvellous, wonderful Romney, all I want to do is to be with you forever and . . . love you."

She paused before she asked a little anxiously:

"You do . . . want my love?"

"I want it more than anything in the whole world!" Lord Heywood answered.

"And you are not . . . angry or . . . resentful because I am . . . wealthy?"

"I suppose it is one of those tiresome things I shall have to put up with!" he replied. "But I daresay it will come in useful in one way or another."

Lalita laughed.

"I know you are going to spend it on the farms and roofs, on pensioners and Alms-Houses."

"I might let you have just enough to buy a new gown now and then," Lord Heywood said, "or one of those provoking and very delectable nightgowns."

The way he spoke made Lalita blush, and then she said:

"You will have to . . . forget until we are . . . married tomorrow that you have ever . . . seen me in one."

"Tomorrow?" Lord Heywood asked. "Why should I want until tomorrow?"

"I . . . I thought," Lalita replied, "that we . . . were to be married . . ."

"Tonight!" he said. "Carter said he would be back before dinner. Go and change, my darling. We will saddle our horses and ride down to talk to the Vicar."

"Do you . . . mean it? Do you . . . really mean it?" Lalita asked.

"Why not?" Lord Heywood replied. "If you think I

can sleep with the communicating door closed between us, you are very much mistaken!"

"It is the most wonderful . . . glorious idea I have ever . . . heard, for us to be married tonight," Lalita said, "but first I must decorate the Chapel."

It struck Lord Heywood that the whole village would be talking about the death of Edward Duncan. It would be best for no-one except the Vicar, whom he would swear to secrecy, to see Lalita or to know of their marriage.

"I think it would be better," he said, "if I went to see the Vicar alone."

"Yes, of course," Lalita replied, "and, darling, I have an . . . idea, if you will agree."

"What is that?"

"I have nothing special in which to be married . . . but I have . . . found your mother's . . . wedding-gown."

"Where?"

"In a cupboard in one of the rooms where there are a lot of other clothes, including some of yours when you were a boy."

"My mother's wedding-gown!" Lord Heywood said reflectively. "Are you sure? And how do you know it will fit you?"

Lalita looked embarrassed.

"You have tried it on!" he said accusingly.

"Just in . . . case . . . you . . . did marry me."

"And now I have decided to do so."

"Please . . . please . . . I want to look . . . beautiful for you just . . . in case you . . . change your . . . mind."

"I shall not change my mind, my alluring love, whether you marry me in my mother's wedding-gown or your very revealing nightgown, but I think the Vicar will prefer you in the former."

"There is a wreath and a veil with it . . . and I want to feel really . . . married."

"I will convince you of that, my beautiful bride, but get the gown ready and start picking the flowers. I will not be away for more than half-an-hour, then I will help you with them."

Lalita gave a cry of joy.

"I will go and pick all the carnations from the green-houses and of course plenty of roses."

"Which are like you," Lord Heywood said in his deep voice. "I have always thought of you, my precious, as being like a white rose, pure, untouched, and—for the moment—in bud."

There was something in the way he spoke which made Lalita feel as if little shafts of sunshine were running down her spine.

"I love . . . you!" she whispered.

"And I love you!" Lord Heywood replied. "And I will explain how much and how deeply I adore you once you are my wife."

As he finished speaking his lips sought hers, and he kissed her until she felt, as she had before, that the whole world vanished and there was neither the earth nor the sky, but only the strength of his arms, the insistence of his lips, and him.

He awoke a rapture which ran through her with the speed and sharpness of lightning, and yet it was warm and golden like the sunlight.

It rose from her breasts up into her throat to touch her lips and become a fire which was part of the fire burning in him.

It was like the music of angels and the beauty of the

stars, and yet it was as protective as Lord Heywood's arms.

Only when she felt that nobody could experience such ecstasy and not be in Heaven did he raise his head.

"How could I ever lose you," he asked unsteadily, "when you are part of me? You have crept into my life and now it would be impossible to live without you."

"That is what I . . . want you to . . . feel," Lalita answered, "because I know that if I had to live . . . without you . . . I would only . . . want to . . . die!"

"Instead of which we will be together," Lord Heywood said, "and there is so much to do—and now I am using an instinct that is as good as yours—that it will be impossible for two people to be happier."

"I will . . . make you . . . happy," Lalita promised, "and, darling, wonderful Romney, as I told you before, you are the victor . . . the conqueror . . . and you always . . . win."

"I think if we are honest," Lord Heywood replied, "it is love which has won, and love is an emotion against which we have no defence."

"None at all!" Lalita agreed happily. "And please, because I love you . . . so much . . . kiss me again, because your kisses are more perfect, more marvellous, and more exciting than those which have been in . . . my dreams."

Lord Heywood tried to reply, but Lalita's lips were close to his.

She was so lovely, so soft, so feminine that he felt the blood throbbing in his temples, and his whole body was burning with an urgent desire to make her his.

But he knew what he felt for Lalita was so much more than a physical sensation.

What he had never felt for any other woman was a

reverence which made her part not only of his heart but of his soul.

Because of her he would strive not only to make her happy but to make himself more worthy of her love.

He wanted to tell her so, to put his feelings into words, but instead he kissed her, knowing as he did so that fiercely and demandingly they both touched the Divine.

As Lord Heywood felt Lalita surrender herself completely to the insistence of his lips, he knew she was right.

He had won the last battle of his life and been victorious.

It was love—the love that Lalita had given him and aroused in him—which had made him the winner.

"Love wins!" he wanted to say, but Lalita had always known that.

ABOUT THE AUTHOR

BARBARA CARTLAND, the world's most famous romantic novelist, who is also an historian, playwright, lecturer, political speaker and television personality, has now written over 300 books.

She has also had many historical works published and has written four autobiographies as well as the biographies of her mother and that of her brother Ronald Cartland, who was the first Member of Parliament to be killed in W.W. II. This book has a preface by Sir Winston Churchill and has just been republished with an introduction by Sir Arthur Bryant.

Barbara Cartland has sold 200 million books over the world, more than half of these in the U.S.A. She broke the world record in 1975 by writing 23 books and the four subsequent years with 20, 21, 23 and 24. In addition her album of love songs has just been published, sung with the Royal Philharmonic Orchestra.

Barbara Cartland, who is a Dame of the Order of St. John of Jerusalem has championed the cause for old people and founded the first Romany Gypsy Camp in the world.

Barbara Cartland is deeply interested in Vitamin Therapy and is President of the British National Association for Health. Her book the *Magic of Honey* has sold in millions all over the world.

She has a magazine, *The World of Romance*, and her Barbara Cartland Romantic World Tours will, in conjunction with British Airways, carry travelers to England, Egypt, India, France, Germany and Turkey.

Barbara Cartland

The world's bestselling author of romantic fiction. Her stories are always captivating tales of intrigue, adventure and love.

☐	20013	RIVER OF LOVE	$1.95
☐	14503	THE LIONESS AND THE LILY	$1.75
☐	13942	LUCIFER AND THE ANGEL	$1.75
☐	14084	OLA AND THE SEA WOLF	$1.75
☐	14133	THE PRUDE AND THE PRODIGAL	$1.75
☐	13032	PRIDE AND THE POOR PRINCESS	$1.75
☐	13984	LOVE FOR SALE	$1.75
☐	14248	THE GODDESS AND THE GAIETY GIRL	$1.75
☐	14360	SIGNPOST TO LOVE	$1.75
☐	14361	FROM HELL TO HEAVEN	$1.75
☐	14585	LOVE IN THE MOON	$1.95
☐	13985	LOST LAUGHTER	$1.75
☐	14750	DREAMS DO COME TRUE	$1.95
☐	14902	WINGED MAGIC	$1.95
☐	14922	A PORTRAIT OF LOVE	$1.95